"Son, that sounds like a great idea."

"What does?" Becca stared at Clay in astonishment.

"For me to come live with you again," Clay said with an air of decisiveness.

Becca held her hands up as if she was trying to stop a speeding bus. "No, Clay. No. First of all, I can't imagine that you'd want to...."

"Then you imagined wrong. I'd love to. Thanks for the invitation."

"No, Clay." She hardened her voice. "We'll find someone to take care of you, and..."

"But Mom," Jimmy piped up, "don't you want Dad to come stay with us?"

Becca looked down at her son's puzzled face.

Clay reached out and drew Jimmy to him. "Yeah, Mom, don't you want me to come stay with you?"

Dear Reader,

I've always been fascinated by strong women, which is one of the reasons I love romance novels. MARRIAGE TIES is a series about a family of such women: a mother, her stepdaughter and two daughters. To test their strength, I teamed them up with men who are anything but tame. The Kelleher women are strong, though they don't always know how their strength will be tested. But then, none of us knows until it happens.

In *Another Chance for Daddy*, Rebecca Kelleher Saunders thinks she's sending her six-year-old son off to spend a week with his father, Clay, but fate intervenes. Clay, the husband she thought was out of her life—the man she knew so well—is back. He's not going anywhere, and has he ever changed!

Wedding Bells, to be published in November (#3530), and *Bachelor Cowboy*, due in 1999, tell the stories of Rebecca's sisters, Brittnie and Shannon, and the men who attract these remarkable women. Late in '99, look for *Resolution: Marriage*, the story of Mary Jane Kelleher, the mother to these three women, who is reunited with her high school sweetheart and must come to terms with a secret she's kept for more than twenty-five years.

Be prepared to enjoy the strength and resourcefulness, the fun and the tears, of Rebecca, Brittnie, Shannon and Mary Jane.

Happy Reading!

Patricia Knoll

Another Chance for Daddy
Patricia Knoll

Harlequin Books

TORONTO • NEW YORK • LONDON
AMSTERDAM • PARIS • SYDNEY • HAMBURG
STOCKHOLM • ATHENS • TOKYO • MILAN
MADRID • WARSAW • BUDAPEST • AUCKLAND

ISBN 0-373-03502-0

ANOTHER CHANCE FOR DADDY

First North American Publication 1998.

Copyright © 1998 by Patricia Knoll.

Printed in U.S.A.

CHAPTER ONE

TROUBLE was coming up Rebecca Saunders's front walk. As she looked out the window, she pressed her hands against her stomach, took a deep breath and held it until her nerves steadied.

Trouble was her ex-husband, Clay.

He drove a midnight-blue, four-wheel-drive Ford Explorer that had scattered gravel in all directions when it swept into her driveway and parked behind her little green Honda. He had a way of stepping down from the vehicle, stretching a six foot two inch frame until every chest and shoulder muscle rippled beneath a black snap-front shirt, placing a cowboy hat on a head of deep auburn hair and examining the neighborhood through dark green eyes. She knew he had taken in everything at one glance, judged it, and probably found it wanting.

This was not the kind of neighborhood they had ever lived in together. Their apartments had all been in modern buildings lacking in uniqueness, whether they had been located in Louisiana, Texas, or Mexico.

This home and this neighborhood were unique; each house was different, from her own small three-bedroom bungalow to the Emerson's sprawling two-story whose trim had recently been painted hot pink. This was the kind of neighborhood where she had always wanted to live, but Clay hadn't. He had never wanted the responsibility and upkeep of a home. Besides, he had said, a house would be too hard to sell when they moved on to his next job—a statement that had always made Becca's heart sink to her toes because she had feared his attitude would never change—and it hadn't.

As she watched, he walked down the driveway to her front gate, then strolled along the brick sidewalk with a leisurely pace.

He looked over her yard, at the brown grass that would turn green in a few weeks, the forsythia and rose-bushes that rattled dry branches against the picket fence, and the flower beds where crocuses were poking their first tentative green shoots through the rich brown soil as if sending up scouts to see if winter truly was finished.

Even as she berated herself for doing it, she searched Clay's face for signs of approval, but saw only mild interest.

Then she studied his face because in the past it had given her so much pleasure to do so. It was a strikingly handsome face with deep-set eyes, a long, straight nose, and a rarely-seen grin. She used to love that grin. It had always seemed like a gift when it appeared. At one time it meant laughter, fun, good times. She didn't see that grin now. In fact, she never saw it. There was nothing of laughter, fun, and good times between them now.

Becca stood behind her lace curtains, knowing that she was acting cowardly, that she should throw the door open and invite him right in. After all, he had called ahead, made all the necessary arrangements. This visit wasn't a surprise. She had thought she was prepared; she had been up cleaning house since six that morning to work off her nervousness, but it plagued her with butter-flies beating frantically inside her.

Becca had moved out almost a year and a half ago. Their divorce had been final for six months. She wondered how much longer it would be before she stopped having this physical reaction to him—this burning sensation that swept up from her stomach to her throat and then her face. True, she was still attracted to him. What red-blooded woman wouldn't be? But that wasn't the reaction she was having now. It almost felt like embarrassment, but she had nothing to be embarrassed about. She had done what was best for herself and Jimmy, who was then barely five years old. She had moved the two of them back to her hometown of Tarrant, Colorado.

Clay had fought the divorce, as she had known he would, but she had held her ground until the final decree had been granted and she had been free to start life again, this time as a single mother. She had family in Tarrant; her stepmother and her half-sisters, aunts, uncles, and cousins. It was home, and it was safe and comfortable. She needed a secure routine and some emotional comfort after her years with Clay.

She had certainly achieved a secure routine, but little emotional comfort of any kind and she felt it anew every time she saw him now.

There had been bitter words, hard feelings, and trouble in general between her and Clay ever since she had left him. However, when he had called a couple of weeks ago, Clay had asked for a truce. He was going to be leaving the country soon to take an engineering job in Venezuela and would be gone for several months. He wanted to have Jimmy during the youngster's spring break from school. They were going skiing. Clay apologized for the hard time he'd given Becca since the divorce, saying that he now realized the whole situation would be much easier for Jimmy if he knew his parents were on friendly terms.

Becca had been so relieved by this overture of peace, that she had immediately agreed to the skiing trip. Now

Clay was here, and she hoped she hadn't made a terrible mistake.

She heard his boots on the front porch, then his knock on the door. Before she could prepare herself any further, or give herself a pep talk about seeing him face-to-face, a whirlwind in the form of her son whipped by her.

"I'll get it. It's Dad. I saw him from my window," Jimmy shouted as if his mother had suddenly been struck with deafness.

Excitedly, he wrestled the door open, then leaped straight into the air and into his father's outstretched arms, shouting, "Daddy, you came. I knew you'd come."

"Hey, I wouldn't let my guy down. You know that." Clay's deep voice was muffled as he buried his face against Jimmy's neck.

Standing in her living room and watching the tender scene in the doorway, all Becca could see was the top of Clay's black Stetson. It obscured Jimmy's head, too, so that the only things visible were his little back and his short, jeans-clad legs. Clay's arms were wrapped tightly around his waist.

Becca's eyes filled with tears and she turned her head away as she blinked them back. Clay and Jimmy had always been close. Even though he'd never been around an infant before his son's birth, Clay had never balked at the diaper-changing and floor-walking associated with a baby—and Jimmy had been a sick, fussy baby. She wanted to see that closeness continue even though it meant that she would have extended contact with Clay herself.

When Clay pulled away from Jimmy and lifted his head, Becca braced herself. In spite of his request for a truce, she expected to see censure in his eyes as she had for the past two years. Instead, they were cool and guarded, as was his smile.

"Hello, Becca. How are you?" he asked as his gaze traveled over her, taking her in, from her long chocolate-brown hair, which was pulled back into a neat French braid, to the steady look in her aquamarine eyes, to the set of her full lips and the angle of her narrow chin.

As he examined her, Becca was glad that she had foregone her usual loafers, jeans, and sweater for her dressy boots and a calf-length dress of soft sky-blue flannel. It helped to know that she looked her best.

"I'm fine, Clay," she answered, and was quite pleased with the cool confidence in her tone. "Come on in," she invited with a sweep of her hand. "Jimmy's been up since the crack of dawn, watching for you."

Clay's right eyebrow rose a fraction. "I'm here exactly when I said I would be."

"Yes, yes, of course," she said hastily. "It's just that he doesn't tell time very well yet. He's only in the first grade, you know." She was *not* going to mention the number of times that work had made him break promises to Jimmy, or to her. Nor would she let him think that she had been speaking badly about him to his son. "I told him you would be on time, but he didn't really understand when ten o'clock would arrive." Becca stopped suddenly, realizing that she was babbling.

She stepped back and her hand fluttered out. "Why don't you sit down for a few minutes? Jimmy just learned to read his first book on his own and his teacher let him keep it over spring break so he could read it to you." She glanced down at her son, who was now clinging to his father's leg. "Honey, why don't you go get your book now? Since it belongs to the school library, you can't take it on your trip with you, but you can read it to your dad before you go.''

Jimmy grinned up at her, showing a gap where his new front teeth were coming in. His hair and eyes were so much like Clay's that sometimes it hurt. He occasionally had Clay's stubbornness, too, but today he was all smiles. "I'll bring my gear, too.''

Jimmy turned and ran off, taking with him the whirlwind of excitement that followed him everywhere.

Becca gestured for Clay to sit on the sofa. See? she told herself. This could be easy if they both worked at it. Their meetings didn't have to degenerate into the hot words or cold silences of the past. Those silences had been her greatest frustration in their marriage. She came from a family that talked out, even yelled out, their problems. Except in moments of passion, Clay had never shown his deepest emotions.

Becca gave herself a mental shake. She didn't know why she was thinking about Clay and moments of passion. In fact, she didn't know why she was going over any of this now, except that every time she saw him, the unresolved feelings surfaced.

Becca forced a smile. "Jimmy's packed and repacked his duffel bag six times,'' she said. "There's no telling what you're going to find when you open it.''

"Just so he has his ski clothes and boots.''

"He does.''

Clay sat after he had removed his hat and placed it upside down on the coffee table. He stretched his long legs out, extended his arm along the back of the sofa, and relaxed. Becca perched nervously on the chair opposite, wishing she could be at ease the way he was. After all, this was her house, the kind she had always wanted when they were married. The living room was comfortable with its deep, overstuffed sofa and chairs upholstered in blue and cream checked fabric, the big window swagged with lace and muslin, and the touches of country charm that decorated the walls, bookcase, and tables. She'd had one of her cousins, a carpenter, build plate rails and shelves along the top of the wall in the dining room to display her collection of pre-Depression glassware.

Becca cleared her throat and gave him a bright smile. In spite of her best efforts she knew it looked as fake as a three dollar bill. "I'm quite pleased with Jimmy's teacher this year. She puts a real emphasis on reading and math. He's doing very well."

Again, Clay gave her that steady look, which was beginning to unnerve her. "Yeah, I figured that out from the copy you sent of his report card."

"Oh, oh, of course." Becca's heart sank. This was harder than wading through cold molasses.

She turned her head and looked out the window at the clear March sky. There had been a time when conversation between them had flowed easily and naturally. They had been able to talk about anything—or so she had thought. She realized now that their conversations had never really dealt with the overwhelming differences between them—his need for adventure and hers for safety and security. Their conversations had certainly never touched that secret place that Clay had always kept locked away from her.

Clay, a mining engineer, had been working on a short-term contract for an oil and gas company. The company's owner had taken Clay to discuss a possible easement for a gas line across her father's, Hal Kelleher, property. She had been there, too, that day, picking up her youngest sister, Brittnie, for a trip to the orthodontist's in Durango. She had almost missed Brittnie's appointment because once Clay had arrived, she had lingered at the ranch, intrigued and yet terrified by the impact of meeting him.

He had sought her out that night, locating her at her job, managing the local movie theater. He had taken her out and they had talked until nearly dawn, then they'd been together every free minute after that. They had fallen immediately into lust and married after a three-week courtship. At the time, she had thought it was like a fairy tale. She realized now that their speedy marriage had possessed exactly as much substance as a fairy tale.

Even after all this time, the memory of their meeting still brought her intense joy, followed by sorrow. How could they have known things would go so wrong?

Determined to get through this short visit with as much civility as possible, Becca brought her attention back to Clay and discovered that he was studying her with the clear-eyed intensity he brought to everything he did. She met his eyes for a fleeting instant and saw sharp emotion there, but it was gone before she could identify it. His face went blank, as if he was expecting her to make the next gesture. Becca sighed inwardly. She had made all the gestures so far. She had to admit that this was better than fighting with him, but she didn't know what he was thinking. At least when they had fought, she had known what was going on in his mind—somewhat.

Did he feel the same regrets she did? She had no idea and that was basically what had lain at the root of all their problems when they had been married.

"Can I offer you some coffee, Clay?" she asked, and wished her voice sounded less strained.

"Sure," he said. "Thanks."

Relieved to be doing something, Becca hopped up and headed for the kitchen, but was distressed to glance back and discover that he was following close behind her.

"I'll bring it out here, Clay," she said, giving him a fleeting smile over her shoulder.

He answered with a steady look. "You don't have to treat me like a guest, Becca. I can drink coffee in the kitchen."

"All right," she agreed, but she felt an edge of irritation. Why couldn't he make such a simple thing easy? "Won't you sit down?"

She already had the coffeemaker set up, so she flipped the switch to start it brewing, then began getting cups from the cabinet and cream from the refrigerator. When she had fiddled with the preparations as long as she could, she finally turned around, folded her arms across her waist, and wished she could think of something to say.

Clay had pulled out one of the four chairs that went with her oak table and sat now with his long legs stretched out before him and his strong miner's hands resting casually on the polished wood. Glancing at the centerpiece of dried prairie grasses in a squat terra-cotta jug, then at the tabletop beneath his hands, he said, "This is new."

"Yes, it is." She brought their cups to the table, handed him his with just the amount of cream he liked stirred into it, then sat down opposite him. "It's new to me at least. Mary Jane found it in the barn after Dad died. It was my grandmother's. I had it refinished." She wasn't sure why she added that last bit. It wasn't as though he cared. Heirlooms such as her grandmother's table had never meant much to him.

He nodded. "In fact, it looks like you've finally got the place you always wanted."

She listened for censure in his tone, but hearing none, she glanced around at her lovely little home and said, "Yes, I do."

"So things are all set for you, then?"

There was something in his deep voice that made her shift uncomfortably in her chair, then hide her discomfort behind a sip of coffee. "Jimmy has made friends here in the neighborhood and at school. Things are going fine. How about you? When did this job in Venezuela come up?"

"A few weeks ago. George Cisneros called, said they needed me for some preliminary work on a mine they're opening down there." He shrugged. "And now there's no reason for me not to go."

There was no accusation or self-pity in his tone. He was matter-of-fact, but she felt a twist of guilt knowing that their divorce was the reason he was now free to take a job in South America. He'd wanted to years ago, saying the cultural changes would be good for them. Since they both spoke some Spanish, living in South America wouldn't be hard for them. Becca had fought the move, reluctant to be so far from her family for such a long time. Mexico had been a great enough distance for her.

Before she could respond, Jimmy struggled into the room, pulling his overstuffed duffel bag with one hand, and clutching his book with the other. The tip of his tongue peeked from the corner of his mouth and a lock of dark hair flopped over his forehead. Clay started to his feet to help the boy out, but when Jimmy had the bag two inches inside the kitchen, he abandoned it in the doorway and rushed to climb into Clay's lap.

Clay grunted when Jimmy's elbow connected with his

stomach. Rubbing the tender spot, he looked at the book's cover, then gave Becca a questioning glance. "Gems and minerals?" he asked.

"I admit the book's a little thin on plot, but most of it is written at his level, and it's his favorite subject," she said, her eyes sparkling. "He must have inherited it from you."

Clay grinned, the first natural smile she'd seen from him since he had arrived, and she relaxed against the back of her chair. Since she had read, and heard, the book several times already, she sipped her coffee and watched Clay as he helped their son with such words as "feldspar" and "sandstone." She wasn't sure how much of the book Jimmy actually understood, but he loved rocks of all types, was a fount of information about them, and could be counted on to volunteer interesting tidbits at any given moment.

When he finished, Jimmy gave a satisfied sigh, jumped down from his father's lap and dashed away to put the book back in his room.

"His teacher said he's the only child to check that book out of the school library in two years. He's kept rechecking it every week for a month. He should have it memorized by now."

Clay nodded, then smiled at her with such pride in his son, that Becca felt tears clog her throat. This is the way it should always be between them, sharing in their son's accomplishments.

"We went up to the old Lucy Belle mine a few weeks ago," she continued when she knew she'd conquered the tears. "He was convinced he could find gold there, even thought it was a silver mine. He had on a pair of sweatpants with big pockets that he filled so full of rock samples the seat hung down past his knees. He walked around all day with his feet wide apart to keep his pants from falling down. He looked as if he was saddle sore, but he couldn't bear to leave even one rock behind. He was sure they were pure gold.''

Clay smiled again, then his face grew thoughtful. ''You two didn't go up there by yourselves, did you? Those old mines are pretty dangerous, rotting timbers, standing water....''

''We weren't alone,'' Becca broke in hastily, then busied herself picking up her coffee cup and carrying it to the sink. ''We were with Barry,'' she added in a tone that she hoped sounded casual. ''Would you like more coffee?'' She had the feeling, though, that she resembled someone who, when meeting a bear in the woods, throws a decoy in one direction and runs in the other praying for a distraction while hotfooting it toward safety.

''Barry Whelker? Your boss?'' Clay's tone was deceptively soft. ''Is he interested in abandoned mines?''

Becca turned to face him, her back to the sink and her hands behind her, gripping the edge of the ceramic tile counter. ''Not very much. But he knows Jimmy is.''

''Why should he care?''

''He's a nice man,'' she said carefully.

Clay's mouth firmed into a straight line. ''So you've said, but why does he care about Jimmy's interests?''

Her eyes darted away, then back to meet his. Her chin came up. ''You see, Clay, Barry and I have been dating.''

''Dating?''

His voice had dropped to a low rumble. Becca swallowed hard and told herself she wasn't afraid of him, or of his reaction. Her social life really wasn't any of his business. ''Yes, you remember dating, don't you? It's that getting-to-know-you activity we didn't do enough of before we got married."

"I see, and you're taking my son along on these dates?" Clay rose from his chair and leaned forward, the tips of his fingers resting on the tabletop. His eyes had gone as dark as the sea before a storm.

"Occasionally, if it's a family activity...."

"But not on the private activities between the two of you?"

Anger flushed Becca's face red, brought her hands to her waist and her chin higher into the air. "Just exactly what are you implying, Clay?"

"I'm not *implying* anything. I'm asking if you're being careful around Jimmy."

"We're certainly not doing anything wrong, Clay, and furthermore, I don't see why you would think it was any of...."

The back door flew open and banged against the wall, startling them both. They whirled around to see Becca's youngest sister, Brittnie struggling into the room. Her arms were full of a large scrapbook and several photograph albums. A small baker's box rode precariously on top. Her face was turned away as she steadied the box against her cheek.

"Hi, Sis," she huffed, reaching behind her with her foot to shut the door against the March breeze, and at the same time, making a grab for the sliding box. "I picked up the stuff you wanted from Dan's Bakery. His wedding cakes are the best in town. He sent a photo album of his best cakes and a sample of the lemon one. I had the chocolate one last year at Brenda Luna's reception. It was wonderful. I think you and Barry will be happy with any of them." Abandoning her struggle with the door, she turned around and said, "Hey, can you help me out here? I've got my hands full, you know, and you're just standing there like your shoes are nailed to the..." Her eyes widened and her voice trailed off when she spotted Clay. "Floor," she finished in a sinking tone. She darted a quick glance at Becca, licked her lips and said meekly, "Hi, Clay."

"Hello, Brittnie." He straightened away from the table and moved toward her with a smooth, gliding stride that made Becca think of a stalking panther. "What did you say you've got there?"

Brittnie, whom Becca had always considered to be the fast thinker in the family, whipped around, dumped the articles on the counter behind her sister, then stood shoulder to shoulder with her and gave her former brother-in-law a big, empty-headed smile. "Oh, nothing, just some...Oh, nothing."

Clay stood before the two of them and tried to peek over their shoulders. "What was all the talk about wedding cakes?"

"Dad, I put my book away," Jimmy shouted from the living room. His pounding feet were fast approaching the kitchen. "Can we go now?"

When he skidded to a halt in the doorway, Becca looked at his expectant face, then threw a frantically pleading glance at Brittnie, who leaped away from the counter and swooped toward her nephew.

"Hey, Sport," she said cheerily. "Your mom and dad need to have a little talk. Why don't you show me your rock collection?" Over his loud protests, she swept him into her arms.

"You already saw my rock collection," he insisted, arching away from her and giving his parents an anxious look. "Are Mom and Dad gonna have a fight?"

"No, no, of course not," Brittnie assured him though

her voice had an edge that said she didn't believe that, either.

"'Cause I don't like it when they fight."

"They won't fight," she reassured him as she hustled him away.

In the kitchen, Becca stared at Clay, as fascinated as a cobra held fast by a mongoose. Bit by bit, the polite but cool expression he had worn for the past half hour crumbled away as if a stone mask was being chipped off.

His eyes darkened, his thick brows drew together like gathering thunderclouds and his jaw tightened. "Wedding cakes, Becca?" he asked in a silky tone. "Now just why would you be interested in wedding cakes? And why would Barry be interested in wedding cakes right along with you?"

Becca felt as if her heart had dropped to her stomach, then bounced back up again. Now it was stuck behind her esophagus, cutting off her air. She cleared her throat and opened her dry mouth to speak, but it was a moment before anything came out.

"We...uh, we...he...'re getting mar...married," she wheezed, stretching the words out, then could have kicked herself for reacting as if she'd been caught doing something wrong.

"Married?" he asked, moving to stand towering over her. "You and Barry?"

"That's...that's right."

"This is the first I've heard of it, Becca. In fact, I just learned five minutes ago that you two are dating."

"Well, well, we are," she bluffed, holding her chin at such an exaggerated angle that she feared her jaw would crack. "I've been dating Barry for three months now."

"And now you're going to marry him?"

"That's right. We...we just made the decision a few days ago." Finally, her fear of his reaction began to fade and her natural stubbornness kicked in. "And frankly, I don't see that this is really any of your business, Clay."

"The hell it isn't. Anything that affects my son is my business and your remarriage will definitely affect him. What does he think of this, by the way?"

Becca glanced away. "He likes Barry."

"That doesn't answer my question." Clay reached out, snagged her chin between his thumb and forefinger and forced her to look at him. "What does Jimmy think about having Barry for a stepfather?"

Although the rough callouses on his thumb chaffed her skin, Becca didn't pull away. She met his eyes steadily.

After a moment, Clay's eyes widened in shock, his hand dropped to his side and he said, "I'll be damned. You haven't told him yet, have you?"

"No, I haven't."

"Why the hell not?"

Now she was losing her defensiveness and getting angry, too. "Don't swear at me, Clay. I haven't told him yet because I was waiting for the right moment."

Clay's hands rose slowly to his waist and his jaw thrust forward belligerently. "And just when would that be? Five minutes before you walked down the aisle?"

"Oh, don't be ridiculous. I didn't tell him yet because I didn't want to spoil his skiing vacation with you." Immediately, she knew she had said the wrong thing, but she couldn't backtrack now.

Clay jumped on her mistake like a cat landing on a mouse. "Are you listening to yourself?" he asked in a scoffing tone. "If news of your marriage would spoil his vacation, then it must not be good news."

Becca's hands dropped and curled into fists. "I meant that he would be thinking about it a great deal and not enjoying his time with you." Finally, she just shut her mouth, knowing she was doing nothing but making things worse. She took a deep breath. "Listen, this isn't getting us anywhere. Why don't you go on your skiing trip and have a good time? When you get back, we'll sit down together with Jimmy and explain everything."

Clay stared at her. "Fat chance."

"You said yourself that his reaction to our divorce would be much easier for him if he thinks we're on friendly terms."

"I wasn't talking about this! Besides, why would he think we would be on friendly terms about you marrying again, Bec? We haven't been on friendly terms about much of anything in two years."

"Then it's time we started," Becca snapped.

She longed for him to leave, to let her sit down, rub away the headache that was beginning to pound in her temples and figure out how she had made such a mess of this when she'd had it so carefully planned.

Clay drew away, his hands dropped to his sides where they opened and closed a couple of times as he said, "This isn't the end of this, Becca. You have no right to spring something like this on Jimmy—or on me, for that matter."

He turned and strode from the room, snatching up Jimmy's duffel bag and calling his name as he went. Becca was left to slump against the counter and try to catch her breath.

"Stupid, stupid," she muttered fiercely, thumping the heel of her hand against her forehead. She had to do a better job of handling things like this or her life would continue to be a battleground even after she married Barry, and Jimmy would always be caught in the middle.

When she felt a little steadier, she pulled herself up straight, smoothed her dress, and walked into the living room. Jimmy was giving Brittnie a goodbye hug, but when he saw Becca, he broke away and rushed toward her, anxious to be reassured that everything was okay between his mom and dad, have the goodbyes over, and be on his way.

Quietly, she reassured him that she and Clay had finished their discussion and things were fine. Becca hugged him tightly and kissed him until he wiggled away. "Mom, that's enough kissing," he said, holding her off. "I gotta go. Dad's waiting."

At last, Becca looked up and met Clay's eyes. They were still full of fire laced with accusation that was aimed at her. He had picked his hat up from the coffee table and was slapping it against his leg, his gestures so controlled she knew he was still seething.

From nowhere, guilt washed over her. This time, she couldn't convince herself that she had done nothing wrong.

"Are you okay to drive, Clay?"

He gave her a look that asked if she was kidding and said, "We'll be back Saturday night." Reaching into his pocket, he pulled out a slip of paper. "Here's the number where you can reach us."

She took it from him. "All...all right. Thank you."

Becca looked at him as Jimmy opened the front door and began dragging his duffel bag onto the porch and Brittnie slipped away to the kitchen. Probably to see if it was still standing, Becca thought.

This is the place where, in the past, she would have

thrown herself into Clay's arms and clung to him, hating the weakness in her that seemed to demand that everything be smoothed out between them before he left. This is when he would have kissed her until she was breathless and promised to be home as soon as possible.

They couldn't do that now. They were divorced so such displays were out of the question. Also, there were too many bad things crowding out whatever good had been between them.

She clasped her hands in front of her and rocked on her boot heels as she broke eye contact with him. "Well, I'll be seeing you on Saturday, then, Clay."

With a nod, he placed his hat on his head and strode outside. She followed, watching as he stowed Jimmy's bag in the back of the Explorer, then buckled their son's seat belt securely and climbed in behind the wheel. Jimmy waved excitedly as they backed out. Her answering wave was as cheerful as she could make it. She mouthed "I love you's" to him.

Clay lifted his head suddenly, his eyes locking with hers as the Explorer rolled into the street. He was looking at her, at the way she addressed her love to their son, and that's why he didn't see Joey Emerson's Monte Carlo as it broke over the top of the hill and raced down the street toward them.

CHAPTER TWO

THE hospital waiting room doors flew open and Becca looked up to see Mary Jane and Shannon Kelleher rushing toward her, anxiety in their faces. Relieved, but shaking, she stood to be folded in her stepmother's arms. Although Mary Jane was only thirteen years older than she, Becca, who couldn't even remember the woman who had given birth to her, had always thought of her as her true mother, and her best friend. Her half-sister, Shannon, crowded close. She was taller than the other two women. She put her arms around them both so that the three of them were held tightly together.

Becca gave her sister a welcoming look. She had recently begun a new job with the county government's soil conservation office and she had a very tough boss. Becca was grateful her sister had been able to get away.

"Brittnie called," Mary Jane said, pulling away to look into Becca's pale face and tear-bright eyes. She touched her stepdaughter's cold cheek. "She told us everything. How is Jimmy? And Clay? And the Emerson boy?"

Becca took a trembling breath, beginning to feel steadier now that her family had arrived. "Jimmy bumped his head on the door. He's got a lump above his right eye and he's shaken up, but he'll be fine. Dr. Kress is keeping him here overnight to watch him. They're getting him settled in his room, which is why I'm out here. And Joey Emerson wasn't even scratched. I don't know *how* that happened. Clay is hurt the worst

24

because Joey's car hit directly on his side. He seems to have a concussion and his left leg is broken, but we won't know how badly either of those injuries is until the X rays are finished." She looked around vaguely. "It should be pretty soon."

Mary Jane put her hand on Becca's arm and gently drew her back to the sofa. Becca went willingly, grateful for her mother's calm efficiency. Nothing much seemed to rattle her. Becca had realized years ago that Mary Jane had a core of strength she could only hope to equal someday.

"Have you called Barry?" Mary Jane asked.

"He's out of town today," Becca answered as she sat. "In Denver on family business." She wished he was here. His steady presence and rational thoughtfulness were exactly what she needed right now.

Mary Jane gave her another quick hug. "Maybe you can get in touch with him later. We'll wait with you. Where's Brittnie, by the way?"

"Gone for coffee."

Shannon shuddered as she sat down. "That should bring back some unpleasant memories," she commented with a touch of irony. She tossed her long black hair back over her shoulders and looked at her sister with sympathy in her dark eyes. "It's the worst coffee in the world, but we drank gallons of it when Dad was in here."

"How well I remember," Becca agreed quietly. Her hands fell to rest loosely in her lap as she stared morosely at the floor.

Hal Kelleher had died of cancer three years ago in this very hospital. In many ways it had torn his family apart even as it had drawn them closer together. They had all gone on with their lives. Mary Jane stubbornly clung to their ranch, working it alone, with the occasional help of her daughters, a few members of her extended family, and any good hand she could hire. Both Brittnie and Shannon had finished college and Becca....

Thinking of her firm, no-nonsense father, Becca was fully aware of what he would say if he knew her marriage had broken up. He had adored Jimmy and would have been incensed at the potential harm the divorce might cause the boy. He'd thought the world of Clay, though the two men couldn't have been more different. Hal had been a man with no guile and few secrets. Everyone knew where they stood with him. He had always said that once a person started something, that person had to keep on until it was finished. He wouldn't have approved of the way she had given up on her marriage. And he *really* wouldn't have approved the argument she'd had with Clay just before he'd pulled out of her driveway.

Mary Jane sat beside her and lightly rubbed her shoulders as Becca propped her elbow on the arm of the uncomfortable sofa and put her forehead in her palm as she relived the horror of the moment when she'd seen the Monte Carlo heading straight for Clay. She had thrown her front door open and sped down the walk before the two vehicles had even made contact, frantically yelling Clay's and Jimmy's names. Brittnie had heard her and run from the kitchen.

The instant the accident was over, Brittnie had phoned for the police and paramedics while Becca had wrestled Jimmy's door open to find him crying and disoriented. She had checked the cut on his head, then climbed in beside him to examine Clay, who had been unconscious, his side of the windshield crumpled into his lap and the water from the Monte Carlo's radiator shooting like a fountain into the air, soaking them both through the broken window. Inanely, she noticed his beloved Stetson lying on the floor of the vehicle. It was crushed, soaked, and probably ruined.

Becca looked down at the stains of water and engine coolant that still marked her dress, wondering vaguely if they could ever be washed out. Not that it mattered when she thought about the injuries Clay had suffered.

For an unspeakable moment, she'd thought Clay was dead, and a welter of emotions had blasted through her: terror before she had found his pulse, then bone-melting relief when she had realized he was alive, followed by tenderness when he had groggily awakened, rolled his head against her supporting arm, smiled, and said, "Hi, babe. What's the matter?" Then he'd passed out again.

Clay had drifted in and out as the neighbors had rushed from their homes, Joey Emerson had stumbled, unhurt, from his car, and the emergency vehicles had arrived with sirens blaring and lights flashing.

That had been more than an hour ago and this was the first moment she had found to think about the full impact of what had happened and what *could* have happened to her son and husband. Ex-husband, she reminded herself, realizing that it was an easy label to pin on Clay, but it wasn't nearly as easy to hang that label on her feelings for him—especially after today's trauma.

Becca looked up as she heard Brittnie bustling back into the room, grateful for the interruption of her troubled and confusing thoughts.

"Hi, Mom, Shannon," she greeted them as she set two cups of coffee on the low table that stood in front of the sofa. "Here, Becca. Try some of this coffee. I know it looks like axle grease, but it might help perk you up."

"Either that, or she'll be awake all night," Shannon responded, eyeing the black stuff.

"She will be anyway," Brittnie pointed out.

She sat beside Shannon. With her dark blonde hair and lively gray eyes, she looked like the smaller, sunnier version of their father. She liked short skirts, music and dancing and fun of all types. If there was any fun to be had, Brittnie would be in the center of it. She had recently graduated from college with a degree in library science, but she certainly didn't fit the stereotype of a librarian. She was far more likely to be the one making noise than the one quieting the noisemakers.

Becca took a sip from the foam cup. It tasted as bad as she remembered, but at least it gave her something to do with her hands. At the sound of footsteps, she looked up to see Dr. Kress approaching. Setting the cup down shakily, she stood to meet him.

Frank Kress was a tall, affable man in his fifties. He had a warm manner, but when he was worried about a patient, he became brisk and blunt. Becca braced herself and searched his face to see if it betrayed his mood. She remembered the staccato rap of his voice when he'd told them Hal Kelleher couldn't live through the night—and the tears in his eyes when he spoke the words.

"Ah, Becca, there you are," he said, spying her.

She felt herself relax when he gave her a slight smile and sat down in one of the chairs. He flexed his shoulders, rolled his head from side to side and gave a great sigh. "Well, honey, your menfolk have been mighty lucky. Jimmy's going to have a headache for a couple of days and will probably whine about it the whole time. Clay has a concussion that needs to be watched carefully for at least a week and his leg is broken in two places. I've casted it, but he'd better take care of it or risk permanent injury. He's got to stay here for a few days, then he can go home."

Becca stared at him. "Home?" Clay had no home. He'd given up the apartment he had in Boulder. His furniture had been put in storage, the few belongings he carried with him from job to job had no doubt been packed and shipped to Venezuela. She knew exactly what arrangements had been made because she had been part of such moves for five years.

Becca shot a quick glance at her mother and sisters whose concerned expressions matched her own.

"Yes, home," Dr. Kress continued gruffly. "I don't know where that is for him, and I've already told you my opinion of this damned divorce. If your dad was alive he'd probably tan both your hides."

Becca did, indeed, know his opinion. He'd expressed it in great detail when he'd treated her for bronchitis in January, then again when she'd had her annual physical last week.

"Don't worry, Frank," Mary Jane said, stepping forward and touching his shoulder. "We'll take care of it."

The doctor stood and gave a satisfied nod. "Good," he said. "I was hoping I could depend on you. You can see Clay in a little while."

After Dr. Kress had left, Becca gave her mother and sisters a despairing look, then sat down heavily on the sofa. "Clay can't go back to Boulder. He gave up his apartment. He has no family to take care of him while he recovers. He is due to leave for Venezuela at the end of next week."

"Doesn't sound like he's going to make his flight," Brittnie said in a dry tone.

Mary Jane looked at all three of her daughters, then

focused on Becca. "He can come out to the ranch. I'll take care of him."

Becca stared at her. "Absolutely not. You're right in the middle of calving, soon you'll be moving the herd... There's no way you could take on a patient—and believe me, Clay is not the best of patients."

"Yes," Shannon broke in. "I remember the time he sprained his wrist. He couldn't drive, work, or even cut his own meat."

All four women winced in unison. They remembered all too well because it had happened on a visit home to the ranch. They had all suffered his bad temper together. They had understood that his surliness was due to his reluctance to be dependent on anyone, but that hadn't made it easier to bear.

Before they could continue the discussion, a nurse approached and said Becca's son was asking for her. With a quick wave to her family and a promise that she would come for them when they could see Jimmy, she hurried off to the pediatrics ward of the small hospital.

In his room, Jimmy sat up in bed, looking about with a frightened expression and tear-filled eyes. When he saw Becca, he started crying. She folded him into her arms and murmured reassurances. After a few minutes he calmed down so she eased him back against the pillow and kissed him.

"Where's my daddy?" he asked as Becca stroked his dark hair away from his face.

"He's in another room."

"Well, tell him to come here. I wanna see him," her son insisted in a petulant tone.

"He was hurt in the accident, too, remember? He has to stay in his bed."

Jimmy moved restlessly. "I wanna go see him in his room."

"Jimmy, honey, I haven't even seen him myself yet."

"Is he dead?"

"No, no, of course not." Becca knew that her son still had vague memories of his grandfather's death and even though he didn't know exactly what death meant, he knew he didn't like the way it made him feel when someone died.

"You and me can go see him."

Becca sighed. She knew he wouldn't rest until he had seen Clay and been reassured that he was all right. "I'll go see if he feels like talking to us, but first I'll get Grandma and Shannon and Brittnie to come in here with you."

"Okay," he agreed. At last, he lay against the pillows and closed his eyes. Becca hurried off to summon her mother and sisters, and while they sat with Jimmy as he began to drift off to sleep, she went in search of Clay's room.

She found him in another wing of the hospital. He was asleep. There was a bandage across the cut on his forehead and his right eye was swollen. The cast on his leg came up to his thigh and was propped up in a sling over the bed to relieve pressure on his hip.

Becca paused in the doorway, then entered slowly, her gaze fixed on him. For some reason, her mind insisted on conjuring up the image of a fallen warrior, which was ridiculous. He was a mining engineer, not a soldier. Still, the image lingered in her mind.

Becca was glad to see that the other bed in his room was empty and she wouldn't be disturbing anyone else by pulling up a chair and sitting for a few minutes while she waited for him to wake.

Wearily, she sank into the chair and stretched her feet out in front of her. It was such a relief to sit calmly after the fright and worry of the past two hours and to know that both Clay and Jimmy were going to be all right. She didn't know what they were going to do about finding a place for Clay to recover. As she had reminded her family, he had no one else. He'd never known his father and had been abandoned by his mother before his tenth birthday to be raised in a series of foster homes. After he'd reached adulthood, he'd made no effort to locate his mother or any member of her family.

When Jimmy was a baby, she had tried to convince Clay to contact his mother, but he had refused. He wanted nothing to do with her. Becca had been very disturbed by his adamant denial that his mother had any rights to know her grandson. He'd refused to discuss his reasons or listen to her arguments.

That had been only one of the many things wrong with their marriage, she thought sadly. They hadn't discussed things. When a problem arose, Clay either took care of it on his own or clammed up about it. She was accustomed to a family who talked things over—often at loud volume—and he was used to handling everything himself. Neither of them had been able to change.

She knew when he woke up, he was going to be difficult. When they had been married, he had rarely been sick and if he was, he had wanted only to be left alone. He hated being dependent on anyone, especially her, now that they were divorced.

Watching him in his helplessness, she felt a flurry of emotions she couldn't quite sort out. She had long ago come to accept the reality that a small part of her would always love him. After all, he was the father of her son. Jimmy's self-confidence and perseverance were traits he had inherited from Clay.

Jimmy had always been the kind of child who liked to do things for himself. In fact, his first words had been "By myself." Clay was the same way—complete unto himself.

She often worried that the closeness she now shared with Jimmy would change over the years until he was closed off to her as Clay was. She dreaded that day.

Along with the love she still felt for Clay, she experienced sorrow and regret, but overriding it all was relief that their battles were over. She had a new life now and soon she would be sharing it with calm, predictable Barry in a permanent home of her own.

She cast Clay a guilty glance. She knew she should have told him about her engagement to Barry, and she certainly should have told Jimmy. It was pure cowardice on her part that she hadn't done so, but she hadn't wanted to argue with him again. They'd argued anyway, and look what had come of it.

Becca started when the phone rang and she grabbed it quickly so it wouldn't wake Clay. He stirred, though, and she picked up the phone and moved as far from him as possible. Cupping the receiver close to her mouth, she answered in a near whisper. "Hello?"

"Rebecca?" Barry Whelker's voice came over the line.

"Barry," she said in relief. "I'm so glad you called. How did you know where to find me?"

"I couldn't get you at your house, and there was no answer at your mother's, so I got your neighbor's number from directory assistance. They told me what had happened. How are Jimmy and Clay?"

Becca smiled, feeling steadied by the even tone of his

voice. Trust Barry to show his resourcefulness in tracking her down and his thoughtfulness by calling her right away. Such thoughtfulness was one of the things she found most appealing about him, both as a boss and a fiancé.

"They're going to be all right," she said. While Barry listened and made concerned sounds, she rapidly ran through a description of Jimmy's and Clay's injuries.

Immediately, Barry offered to come home and help out, but Becca convinced him that her mother and sisters were on hand. There was no need for him to cut short his visit to his family and return before Monday.

"But you'll need my help," he said.

"No, really, Barry," she said, casting a glance at Clay. She could just imagine what her ex-husband would have to say if her fiancé showed up to help her and her family care for him. "It might be better if I don't see you until I've decided what I'm going to do. Clay will need someone to take care of him for a few days at least, and I don't know where that's going to be...."

"But he won't want me around," Barry finished for her.

"Yes, I'm sorry, but it's true," she admitted. "Clay isn't the easiest of men," she said, dropping her voice even more, though her ex-husband still showed no sign of waking up.

"Which is why you're marrying me."

Barry's tone wasn't smug, or triumphant, merely matter-of-fact, which bothered Becca somehow. "Yes, well, that's true," she answered. "But it's not the only reason I'm marrying you."

Barry was silent and she knew that he was thinking about what they both knew—that she didn't love him the way she had loved Clay. She also knew he was too tactful to point that out. She could think of no reply.

Barry finally broke the silence by saying he would call again later and that he would be home in two days.

Becca hung up and sat for several minutes staring at the phone. She felt as though she had somehow disappointed him, but what she had said was true. At the best of times, Clay wasn't an easy man. With multiple fractures and a concussion, he was going to be impossible. She and Barry would soon be sharing the "for better or for worse" of marriage. As far as she could see, there was no reason to start out "for worse."

Quietly setting the phone on the nightstand, Becca turned to look at Clay. It seemed as though she could barely see the movement of his chest as he breathed and she thought of all the times she had worried and feared he was going to be injured on a job site. He'd never received so much as a scratch. Now he'd nearly been killed backing out of her driveway. Shakily, she sat down beside the bed and resumed her vigil.

As she watched, his eyes fluttered open, skimmed over her blankly, then closed again. After a moment, they opened again and stared at her for several seconds. A chill of fear washed through her. It was as if he didn't recognize her, she realized as he drifted off again.

She thought suddenly of how he'd greeted her when he'd momentarily regained consciousness after the wreck. He'd called her "babe," though he'd never been one for endearments. It touched her now and tears filled her eyes.

When he stirred again, she stood, bent over him, and rested her fingers lightly on his cheek. This time his eyelids snapped open and he focused on her with a clear and lucid gaze. Recognition leaped into his eyes, then joy such as she had never seen filled his face as he looked at her, studied her expression, then seemed to delve deeper into her eyes. Then he gazed at each of her features, lingering on her mouth, the hair loosening from her French braid and falling around her face, and then the curve of her cheek. For an instant, it was as if he had been stripped of all pretense.

The pleasure and relief on his face made her think of a time they'd gone exploring in a cave that Clay had sworn was safe. She had twisted her ankle and he'd had to carry her out. They'd both been overjoyed when they had stumbled outside and found light waiting on the other side.

Becca shivered at the memory. She didn't know exactly why she had connected that with the look on Clay's face just now.

Heat washed through Becca, flooding her with the same joy she saw in him.

She was reaching for his hand when something in his gaze seemed to click into place. All expression faded. His eyes swept the room and came back to her.

"Becca," he said in a voice that cracked. He tried to clear his throat. "Can I have some water?"

"Of course." She hurried to get him a glass of water, then eased his head up so he could sip it from a straw.

Satisfied, he turned his lips from the drink and said, "What are we doing here?"

She opened her mouth to answer him, but unexpectedly, tears filled her eyes again. Her lips trembled and the tears poured out. "I'm...I'm sorry, Clay...." She didn't know if she was apologizing for crying or for being responsible for his injuries.

"Are those tears for me?" he asked in a faint voice. "I haven't seen you cry since you...."

Becca's eyes snapped to his, unexpected grief washing them. There was no need for him to go on. Either of them could have finished the thought.... "Since your last miscarriage." Becca took a breath and looked away. This wasn't the time to think about that.

Besides, the truth was, she had also cried plenty over Clay in the past couple of years, but she'd never let him see her at it. Even now, she willed her tears away.

Becca fought to control the tremble in her voice and lips. "How are you feeling?"

"Like I've been run over," he said dryly, looking at her from beneath the edge of his bandage.

"Do you remember what happened?"

"Yeah, I was backing out," he answered in a grim tone. "And I got hit. Did you get the number of the truck that hit me?"

She gave him a rueful look. "It wasn't a truck. It was my neighbor's teenage son in his Monte Carlo."

"That settles it. We're never letting Jimmy...." With a groan of shock, he tried to struggle up onto his elbow. "Jimmy! Where...?"

Her hands sprang out to keep him from climbing from the bed. Even with the huge cast on his leg and the supporting sling suspended above, he would have tried it. "He's all right," she insisted, urging him back. Quickly, she told him what Dr. Kress had said about Jimmy. "He wants to see you, though," she concluded. "I told him he could if you felt up to it."

Clay gave her a fierce glance. "Of course I'm up to it. He needs to be reassured."

"I'll go see if I can bring him here."

It took her a while to find Dr. Kress and get him to agree to let her take Jimmy in a wheelchair to see his dad. Finally, the doctor approved the idea saying it would do Jimmy good and he might continue to rest if he wasn't worried about his dad.

"In fact," he suggested, rubbing his chin thoughtfully. "Now that I think about it, I don't see any reason the two of them can't share a room until Jimmy is released."

"Share a room?" Becca asked, eyeing him warily.

"Sure. This is a small hospital, not many patients right now, we can accommodate a boy and his dad. Besides," he added gruffly. "It'll be easier on you than running back and forth between the two rooms."

Becca didn't point out that she hadn't really intended to run back and forth. Since she was no longer Clay's wife, she didn't feel responsible to watch out for him. He was an independent man—boy, was he independent—and he didn't like being coddled. She didn't say it, though, because she knew it wouldn't quite ring true. She had to focus on Jimmy, though. In spite of her own reluctance to move her son, she knew it would be the best thing for him.

She nodded her agreement and within a few minutes, Jimmy was being wheeled through the corridors to Clay's room with her and her family trailing along behind.

Mary Jane, Shannon, and Brittnie each said a few words to Clay, kissed Jimmy good-night and slipped away, leaving Becca to settle into a chair and ponder exactly how this had come about.

"When's Dad gonna wake up?"

Becca tried to ignore the whining tone in her son's voice though it was beginning to annoy her greatly.

"He'll wake up when he's ready," she answered for at least the tenth time.

"When can we go home?"

Dr. Kress wanted to check Jimmy once more before releasing him, but as the doctor on call at Tarrant General, he'd been summoned to deliver a baby. She didn't feel like explaining all that to Jimmy, though, so she just said, "When your dad wakes up."

"Mom, I need a drink," Jimmy went on, not even pausing for breath between one demand and the next.

Becca looked at her son with a growing mixture of frustration, amusement, and despair. She knew he was playing his injuries, minor though they were, for all they were worth. She was delighted that his twenty-four hours in the hospital were almost over so she could take him home. Her only hope was that she wouldn't be tempted to lock him in his room when she got him there and throw away the key. He had been demanding and petulant all morning, exactly the opposite of his usually sunny nature.

"You just had a drink," she said, moving to stand beside his bed. She was exhausted, having slept very little the night before. Her family had insisted she go home and rest and Brittnie had stayed with her, but she hadn't fallen asleep until far past midnight.

"I need another one," Jimmy said.

She picked up the small plastic pitcher and started to pour water into a glass.

"I want orange soda."

"No."

Jimmy stiffened in his bed and his bottom lip popped out. "But my head hurts."

"James Harold," Clay spoke up from the other bed. "Stop annoying your mother. You don't need another drink. Now be quiet."

Becca glanced up and Jimmy subsided as he, too,

looked at his father in surprise. She had thought Clay was still sleeping, as he had been most of the day—though she didn't know how he had slept through Jimmy's demanding bouts of whining.

She turned to him, noting the improved color of his skin and the brightness in his eyes. "Well, good afternoon," she said, cautiously.

One corner of Clay's mouth eased up. "I haven't slept this late since the last time I had a hang...." He glanced at Jimmy. "...nail," he finished, and Becca laughed at the unexpected silliness of his remark.

Jimmy scooted out of his bed and hurried over to get as close as possible to Clay and pepper him with questions. "How come you didn't wake up, huh, Dad? You been sleepin' all day."

"Not all day, son. They keep waking me to make sure this bump on my head didn't really hurt my thick skull. Looks like you've got a bump, too."

"Yeah." Jimmy grinned suddenly. "We're twins."

Clay chuckled and the sound seemed to calm Jimmy. He asked his father more questions and though Becca knew his head must be pounding with pain, Clay answered, reassuring him that they would go skiing another time. Becca wondered uncomfortably how much he remembered of their argument yesterday just before he'd been struck by Joey's car. She didn't relish the thought of opening that discussion again, but she knew Clay well enough to know that once he felt better, he would pursue it like a bloodhound.

Right now, though, her greatest problem was the one she'd been wrestling with since the day before. Where was Clay going to go to recover once he was ready to leave the hospital?

She walked over to the bed and gently urged Jimmy

away. "Honey, Dad needs to rest. His head hurts, too, just like yours has been hurting."

Clay looked up at her and she felt a tingle of surprise when she noted how the bandage that slanted across his brow gave him a rakish appearance. And somehow, the expression in his green eyes seemed more...relaxed.

"I actually feel pretty good," he said, then lifted himself onto his elbow. "Ah, maybe a little weak, though." He lay back down.

Becca stared. She'd *never* heard him admit to a weakness before.

He grinned at her. "I'm glad you're here, Becca."

Becca's jaw sagged. "You're kidding."

"It's good to see you."

She gave him a long look. "Clay, I think you need to rest a little more."

"I feel fine."

He certainly *looked* fine, considering the shape his leg was in, not to mention his head—and the black eye that was going to be spectacular. In fact, if he wasn't so banged up, she would think he looked better than he had in a long time. There was a light in his eyes she hadn't seen in.... She couldn't remember ever seeing it before, and a teasing smile tilted his mouth.

Becca felt her surprise settle into disturbing warmth that thumped down to rest in the pit of her stomach. Unconsciously, she folded her hands at her waist as if to hold it there.

Off balance, the next thing she knew, Jimmy was tugging at her skirt and saying, "Dad's awake so we can all go home now."

She blinked down at his happy face. "What?"

"You said we were waitin' for Dad to wake up so we could go home. So let's go."

"Jimmy, I meant we were waiting so you could see him before I take you home. He can't leave the hospital yet. He's not well enough."

"Oh. Then we can come back and get him tomorrow." Jimmy scurried back to Clay's bed and gave it a quick examination. "Are you gonna need a special bed like this when we get home?"

Clay looked at Becca's stunned face, then back to his son. "No. I'll be able to use a regular bed."

"Like Mom's?"

"Just like Mom's."

The little boy nodded with satisfaction. "Then we'll come back and get you tomorrow and take you home to live with us again."

CHAPTER THREE

"Son, that sounds like a great idea." Clay nodded thoughtfully at Jimmy's suggestion.

"Wha...at?" The word wheezed from Becca's throat as she stared at him in astonishment. "What does?"

"For me to come live with you again," Clay said, settling his back against the pillows with an air of decisiveness. How he managed *that* little trick as pale and weak as he was, Becca didn't know. She did know that she was rapidly losing her grip on the situation.

She held up her hands as if she was trying to stop a speeding bus. "No, Clay. No. First of all, I can't imagine that you'd want to...."

"Then you imagine wrong. I'd love to. Thanks for the invitation." The devil had the nerve to wink his unblackened eye at her!

Wink? Clay? She stared at him for a second, completely losing her train of thought. She had never seen him wink. He wasn't a winking type of man.

He grinned at her as if he was fully aware of how he'd thrown her off her argument.

Becca brought her scattered thoughts together. "No, Clay." She hardened her voice. "We'll find someone to take care of you, and...."

"But, Mom," Jimmy piped up. "Don't you want Dad to come stay with us?"

Becca looked down at her son's puzzled face.

Clay reached out and drew Jimmy to him. "Yeah, Mom, don't you want me to come stay with you?" He spoke to her over their son's head and Clay's eyes were as pitifully soulful as a basset hound's.

Becca opened her mouth, but only a squeak came out. She was too stunned to offer explanations to her son, or to form words to put Clay in his place. In the seven years she had known him, he had *never* been manipulative. He had simply told her calmly and decisively how things were going to be done. Now, however, he seemed to be metamorphosing right before her eyes. Where was this appalling change coming from?

"I know you have to work," he continued when she didn't break her stunned silence. "But I won't be much trouble. Once the doctor lets me have crutches, I'll be handy to have around the house."

"Handy?" Her voice squeaked as it shot up. "In what way?"

"I can help out." He gave her an even look, but mischief lurked in his eyes. "Do things around the house for you."

"On crutches." Now her voice flattened out.

Clay shrugged. "Maybe I can learn to knit."

"Are you kidding?"

"I could learn," he insisted. He lifted his hands and turned them over, front to back as if offering them for her inspection. "You know I've always been good with my hands."

She waved her fingers in the air as if batting his hands away. "I meant, you've got to be kidding about this whole idea. We can't do this. It would never work."

"Never more serious in my life." His gaze was direct and steady, but now there was an edge of challenge there that she couldn't ignore. "And there's no reason in the world it wouldn't work." His gaze slid to Jimmy, who was looking back and forth from one to the other of them. "We have every reason to *make* it work."

A chill ran over her. She had the feeling they were no longer talking about a temporary stay.

"Clay," she finally managed, though she knew she was floundering and forming her arguments badly. "How serious was that bump you got on the head?"

The challenge died from his eyes and he smiled slightly. "Not so serious that my judgment is clouded. In fact, things are more clear than they've been in a long time."

"That's a matter of opinion," Becca muttered.

Clay didn't answer. He waited silently for the force of his will to win her agreement.

"You have no right to do this."

"Maybe not," he answered quietly. "But Jimmy does, and having me come stay is important to him. Can't you see that?"

"Of course I can," she said, with a sour look that told him she didn't need his help in understanding Jimmy. She knew he was right, but she didn't like the way he was handling this, using their son to manipulate her agreement out of her.

She gave her head a swift shake, rattling her good sense back into place. Reaching out, she pulled Jimmy into her arms, then knelt before him and gave his rounded cheek a light kiss. "Yes, honey, your dad can come stay with us." Lifting her head, she looked her ex-husband right in the eye. "Until he can take care of himself."

Clay answered with a smile of his own that had her narrowing her eyes suspiciously.

"So Jimmy has some idea that he and his dad and I are going to be a family again. With me taking care of Clay until he's better.'' Becca gave her fiancé a distressed look, which he met with calm brown eyes.

"And you hadn't anticipated that?"

"No, of course not." Reaching out, she lined her silverware up with the edge of the table, then folded and refolded the napkin in her lap.

It had been three days since the accident. Jimmy had been home for two nights and was feeling fine. So much so that he had gone out to the Kelleher family ranch to spend a couple of days of his spring vacation with Mary Jane. Since he had missed out on the skiing trip with Clay, this was an alternative treat for him, although Becca didn't anticipate him being much help to his grandmother during such a busy season. His absence from home, though, would give Becca time to get her guest room ready for Clay, who would be coming home tomorrow.

The problem was, she hadn't spent time getting the room ready, or doing much else except wander aimlessly around the house, thinking about what it was going to mean to have Clay back in her life and in her home.

She had been so distracted at work that day that Barry had finally suggested she give up on the project she was starting and go home. He was right. If she kept on, the new business directory was going to be a mess of transposed phone numbers.

Barry had picked her up for dinner at their favorite restaurant in Durango, but she couldn't enjoy the atmosphere and wasn't looking forward to the prime rib she had ordered.

"You should have," Barry pointed out.

Becca looked up and blinked. "Should have what?"

"Anticipated having to bring Clay home with you. It's the logical solution."

Becca gave him a disgruntled look. She usually appreciated his levelheadedness, but not tonight. She wanted him to be as distressed as she was, to listen to her complaints and offer sympathy, though she knew that wouldn't solve anything.

"I suppose so," she admitted with a sigh, more to close the subject than to offer agreement.

Barry returned to eating shrimp cocktail in his slow, methodical way. His table manners signified the way he did most things. She often teased him that by the time he had his food salted to his liking, his meat cut precisely and his bread buttered, ready to eat, everyone else at the table was finished with their meal. He took her teasing good-naturedly, saying that his whole family was like that.

He was something of a perfectionist, though he didn't demand that others do things the way he would. He had been hired as head of the Tarrant Chamber of Commerce two years ago and was doing an excellent job of promoting local businesses and drawing visitors to the area. Tarrant was becoming more than the cattle and farming area it had been for years. Now it attracted retirees from all over the west, especially California. Many of the new residents had found Tarrant as a result of the promotions Barry had done. While the new residents brought increased traffic and more students to the local schools, they also brought increased tax revenues. Everyone liked that, so Barry was respected in the community.

He was a quiet man with dark blond hair and serious brown eyes. He wore glasses to correct his nearsightedness and they added to his solemn appearance. He tended toward conservative suits, pale blue and gray shirts, and patternless neckties. He had been endearingly nervous the first time he had asked her out, a few weeks after she had begun working for him. She had felt safe with him from the beginning and had never found herself on the emotional roller coaster ride that had been so familiar during her marriage to Clay.

When Barry looked up, she gave him a faint smile, picked up her fork and slowly began eating her own appetizer.

After she had agreed that Clay could come home with them to recover, Jimmy had been all smiles and excitement and Clay had seemed quietly satisfied. Becca recalled the argument they'd had over her marriage to Barry and found it hard to imagine that he would want to be anywhere near her, even if it would mean spending several weeks with Jimmy.

Before she and Jimmy had left for home that day, Clay had grabbed the phone, called the man who was sending him to Venezuela and explained the situation. Once the matter was settled, he'd hung up the receiver and given Becca a smile that had said, "I'm all yours."

As if that wasn't enough, the driven, dynamic man she'd been married to, who had terrorized her whole family when he'd had a sprained wrist, now turned into a lamb when the hospital personnel appeared—and there were plenty of them around. Everyone from nurses to laboratory technicians dropped by his room to see how he was doing and he charmed them all. The hospital staff members were delighted with him, and even Dr. Kress couldn't say enough good things about him.

Becca stabbed a shrimp and plunked it savagely into the sauce. She would certainly like to know where all that charm had been hiding itself when she had been married to Clay. She had never seen this side of him before, except perhaps in brief snatches.

She felt dazed and confused with the situation and frustrated with Clay. The weeks of his recovery stretched before her endlessly.

"You're probably wondering if this bothers me," Barry said, breaking into her thoughts.

Becca started and looked up. She'd been so involved in her own feelings, she hadn't even considered his. With guilty haste, she answered, "Yes."

"Sure it bothers me," he said. "I don't like the idea of your ex-husband moving in, broken leg or no broken leg, but it sounds like it's pretty important to Jimmy to have his dad there."

"Yes, it is." Becca smiled in relief. He was such a considerate and thoughtful man. She would never have to worry that Barry would do less than what was best for her son, or for her.

"Then you have to do it." Barry continued eating for a few minutes, then he laid his fork down. With the knuckle of his right forefinger, he pushed his glasses up and peered at her in deep concentration. "In fact, it might be easier on you if you took time off from work."

"Took time off?"

"Yes. The new business directory can wait a couple of weeks," he said in a thoughtful tone. "And that's the only big project you're working on right now."

Her own fork clattered onto her plate and a few people glanced around to see what the noise was. Becca barely noticed them. "But, Barry," she sputtered. "I can't take time off to care for Clay...."

He gave her a dry look. "Well, you certainly can't care for him and work, too. You'll run yourself ragged."

Becca gaped at him, her mind trying to absorb the

idea of being home with Clay all day every day, of making his meals once again, of being on the receiving end of his temper when his current good humor wore off and he realized how restricted his movements would be for a while. She couldn't even think about what the confined intimacy would mean. She had been counting on getting away from the house every day, though she hadn't really considered how he was going to care for himself with her gone. Good grief, the man couldn't even stand without help.

She was going to have to rent a wheelchair from the hospital, and in a couple of weeks, crutches. She would have to give him sponge baths until he was well enough to stand up in the shower with his cast wrapped in plastic. She didn't want to bathe him. Even in his injured state, it would reek too much of intimacy and she wasn't sure she could achieve the kind of detachment a real nurse could. One of the few positive things she had anticipated in this situation was the possibility of getting away and going to work each day.

"Before you object," Barry went on. "Let me say this. I know you pretty well by now."

She came out of her shock a bit and smiled at him faintly. "I should hope so, since we're going to be married."

"And I know that you'll carry guilt around for a long time if you don't do this for Jimmy."

"You do know me well," she sighed. She had agonized for months over her decision to leave Clay in the first place and had struggled with guilt ever since. Maybe Barry was right. She had convinced herself that she was doing the right thing by divorcing Clay. She knew it was the best thing for her, if not the best for Jimmy. They couldn't live together. Perhaps Jimmy would see that by the time Clay was better and ready to leave for Venezuela. On the other hand, such understanding might be a great deal to expect from a six-year-old. She had to take the risk, though.

Besides, no matter what had gone on between them in the past, she and Clay shared a son and she cared about Clay's health and well-being for their son's sake.

After a moment, Becca looked up and reached across the table to lay her hand across Barry's. "You're right, as usual. I've got to do this for Jimmy. I'll take a couple of weeks off, just until Clay is able to get around on his own."

Barry nodded, then said, "There's another thing, Rebecca."

"What?"

He studied her face for a few seconds before he answered. "I've never considered myself to be a particularly insightful man, but I can see that you're not over him yet."

Unable to deny it, she looked down at the table. He was right, of course. A woman didn't get over a man like Clay Saunders without a great deal of strenuous effort put into it.

"Maybe having to take care of him for a while will help you," Barry went on.

She looked up with a wry smile. "You mean it'll remind me of how impossibly hardheaded he is?"

"Something like that, yes."

Becca sighed. "I guess you're right."

For the first time, Barry looked a bit uncomfortable, as if he regretted his suggestion. "Fine. Just as long as you remember that when this is all over you're going to marry me."

She squeezed his hand. "I won't forget."

"Good." He nodded, then pulled away as the waiter came to remove the appetizer dishes and deliver their entrées. When he was gone, Barry said, "I want you to be sure you're doing the right thing because, well, I'm not exactly in his league."

Becca frowned. "What do you mean?"

"I've never been the outdoors type. Taking Jimmy to that mine last week was scary, but your ex-husband must go into places like that all the time."

"No, not really," she hurried to reassure him. She couldn't quite decide where this conversation was heading. "Clay's an engineer, Barry, not a hard rock miner."

"Still, I hope you understand I'm not the kind of man he is."

Becca smiled. She had almost thought Barry was doubting himself, but that wasn't it. He was simply making sure there was complete understanding between them. Again, she reached across the table and took his hand. "Barry, that's the point."

He answered with a shrug and a little twist of his lips and they finished their dinner in peace.

"Here you go, Mr. Saunders." Joey Emerson pushed Clay's wheelchair through the living room and down the hallway toward the bedroom while Becca hurried ahead to throw open the door of the guest room. Jimmy, home from his visit to the ranch, trotted along behind, carrying Clay's shaving kit.

"You'll like your room, Dad," Jimmy chattered. "Mom put the TV and the video games in there so we can play 'em all day. We won't ever have to do anything else."

"Sounds great, son," Clay answered, and Becca knew from the strained tone of his voice that he was gritting his teeth against the pain. The ride home in her small car had been hard on him and she was anxious to get him settled into bed.

Jimmy was so excited, he hadn't stopped talking for the entire ride and his voice had reached a pitch and volume that Becca feared would soon begin shattering all the glassware in the house.

"Jimmy, hush now." Becca tried to quiet her son while at the same time standing back from the door so Joey would have plenty of room to maneuver the wheelchair into the small room. She had offered her bedroom to Clay because it would more easily accommodate the wheelchair, but he had refused, saying he didn't want to inconvenience her any further. He had insisted that the guest room would do fine. Since she felt she had been railroaded into caring for him, she had been surprised, but pleased by his willingness to go along with her household arrangement. He had never been particularly demanding about his living quarters—yet another source of conflict between them because Becca had so longed for a pretty home of her own. Now Becca felt he was being truly thoughtful.

Joey helped Clay from the chair to the bed, which Becca had left turned down when she had gone to the hospital to get Clay. Joey had begged to come along and Becca had let him because she knew he was trying to make amends. He'd had his driver's license for less than a month. His father had now taken it away as punishment for Joey's carelessness. His insurance costs were going to skyrocket because of the accident and he would have to get a job to pay for it. She imagined she would be seeing a great deal of him for the next few weeks. As another part of his punishment, Joey's father had placed him at the Saunders's disposal. Becca had to admit the boy was acting humble and eager to please.

Jaw set, sweat popping out on his forehead, Clay leaned on Joey as Becca steadied him from the back, being careful not to press on the bruises that mottled his back and his left side. With much maneuvering, he made it from the chair to the bed, sinking onto it with a grateful look at Joey and a rueful grimace at Becca. She knew what that look meant. He hated being dependent on anyone, but he was accepting this with surprising meekness. Even though she'd seen the change in him at the hospital, Becca still didn't know quite what to make of it.

Once he was settled on the bed and his leg was propped into a comfortable position, Clay fell quickly asleep. Joey parked the wheelchair in the corner of the room and headed for home as Becca ushered Jimmy into the hallway. Her son whispered violent protests.

"I wanna stay, Mom. What if Dad needs something? A drink of water, maybe, or he might want to play video games."

"He's not going to need anything for a while, and he's certainly not going to want to play games. You've got to let your dad rest, Jimmy," Becca insisted, placing her hands on his shoulders and looking into his eyes. "He's not here to play with you. He's here to get well. He's not going to feel like having us around much for a few days yet."

Jimmy's bottom lip stuck out defiantly, but then he brightened. "Yeah, but then after that, I can see him all the time 'cause he's gonna live with us again." With his usual unquenchable energy, he twisted out of her hands, turned and scampered away.

Becca's hands thumped to her sides, and her head fell forward in defeat.

She had tried to make Jimmy understand that Clay's stay would be short-term, but he hadn't understood—or maybe he simply hadn't listened to what he didn't want to hear.

He bounced into his own room, gathered up a fistful of the military action figures he loved and raced toward the front door. "I'm going over to see if Todd can play."

"Don't be gone too...." Becca's voice died away as the front door slammed and she realized she was speaking to the air. "...long."

With humored exasperation, Becca shook her head and walked into the living room. Now what was she going to do? She had been grateful that Barry had given her the time off from work, but with Jimmy gone and Clay asleep, she wasn't sure how she was going to occupy herself.

When she had been married to Clay, she'd had a great deal of time on her hands. She couldn't work because they moved so frequently. Of course, since Jimmy had come along barely ten months after their marriage, she had been busy with him. She had thought there would be other babies, too, but she had miscarried two times, and each recovery had been long and difficult.

Becca shivered and rubbed her hands over her arms. She didn't like to think about the children she'd been unable to carry to term. Even after all this time, it was still too painful. She turned and looked in the direction of the closed bedroom door. Clay had never understood exactly how she had felt and her depression over the miscarriages. After she had healed physically, she still ached deep inside. It was an ache that nothing seemed to help. She realized now that her feelings had been normal, though exaggerated because she'd been feeling sorry for herself over what she perceived as Clay's coldness toward her suffering. They hadn't been able to talk about it and that had only deepened the rift between them.

Becca shivered at the memory even as she reminded herself that was all in the past now.

For the past year and a half, she had been single-mindedly focused on Jimmy, her job, and her new home. There had always been something to do, especially after she and Barry had begun to date. Now she could admit that much of her busyness had been a method of escaping thoughts of Clay.

She'd had little leisure time and now here she was with an afternoon to herself—at least until Jimmy came home and Clay woke up. Shannon had given her a mystery novel and she'd been wanting to read it for weeks. She smiled as she walked to the bookcase. She would get the book, make herself a pot of tea and relax as she sipped and read. Dr. Kress had assured her that Clay would sleep much of the next few days as his body healed. Jimmy started back to school on Monday, so she would have at least part of each day to herself. If she worked this right, it could be the first real vacation she'd had in a year.

"No, the pillow's still not quite right." Clay looked up at her with long-suffering patience as if he was convinced that if he pushed and prodded her enough and gave her enough instructions, Becca would get the pillow behind his back adjusted into the perfect position.

Becca pressed her lips tightly together and wondered what the penalty was in Colorado for stuffing a bed pillow down the throat of a petulant ex-husband. The sentence might not be too bad if she could get a jury of ex-wives.

Her peaceful afternoon hadn't lasted more than half an hour. Clay had awakened needing attention. She knew he should take a pain pill, but he refused to do it, saying he didn't want to depend on them. Instead, he depended on her.

She tweaked the pillow a bit more so that it settled against the small of his back. "Is that better?" she asked for the sixth time.

At last, he leaned back, smiled and said, "Perfect." He gazed at her as if she had just performed a miracle.

She answered him with a sardonic look. "I was beginning to wonder when the real Clay Saunders was going to show his face."

He glanced up innocently. "Why, what do you mean, Becca?"

"I mean you're impossible when you're sick, grouchy as an old bear. In the hospital you were a dream of a patient, but now you're back to being your usual self."

"Meaning impossible?"

She crossed her hands at her waist. "In a word, yes."

Clay rubbed his chin as if he was considering what she had said.

While he thought that over, Becca looked at him. Even though his nap had been brief, he looked better, the grayish pallor having gone from his face and the pain lines softened around his mouth.

"You're right," he said after a moment's reflection.

Becca narrowed one eye at him skeptically. "I am?"

"I was a good patient in the hospital. There was a head nurse there that scared me right out of my open air hospital gown. I was afraid if I crossed her, she'd tan my very susceptible backside."

Becca felt a smile tugging at her lips. "Oh, who's that?"

"Some lady named Marvella Prentiss. Looks like she still believes in bleeding and purging."

Becca snickered. He was right. That described the dour Mrs. Prentiss perfectly.

"But I can be a good patient for you, too, Becca." Clay's voice had gone low as he said it and Becca gave him a quick look. If he had been just about any other man, she would have thought he was trying to flirt with her, but Clay didn't flirt; he was too straightforward and intense, which was what had first attracted her to him—even as it had scared the bejabbers out of her.

She didn't need to start thinking about what had first attracted her to Clay, or what had scared her about him. He might be her ex-husband, but right now, he was nothing but her patient. She blinked uncertainly and cleared her throat. "Well...well, that's good. I'm glad. That will make things much easier."

"I'll do whatever you want me to do, Becca. You give me an order, and I'll obey." His face was as sincere as she had ever seen it, but there was something about his expression that made her think of a fast-talking salesman offering beachfront property in Arizona.

Now she knew he was teasing, though she wasn't quite sure how she recognized it. He'd never been a tease. It was pleasant, though. His eyes seemed to be lit with a brightness she couldn't remember seeing before.

She tilted her head and studied him. "You seem different."

"In what way?"

She shrugged, wishing she'd never said anything. "I don't know how to describe it." She paused. "More...free."

"I've been bumped in the head," he pointed out. "Must have knocked something loose."

"No doubt," she answered dryly, then stared at him, nonplussed. She'd known this wasn't going to be easy, but she hadn't expected him to be so different—even though she'd seen indications of it in the hospital. He even looked different, and it wasn't because he was so banged up. His black eye looked worse than ever today, and his gauze bandage had been replaced by a large adhesive one. In spite of that, his face was lively. His expression had a waiting quality to it as if he was biding his time to see what she was going to do—and he looked as if he was truly enjoying watching her discomfort.

Becca's hands curled into fists. Oh, she didn't need this. She didn't need to be reminded that even bruised and banged up, he was still an attractive man, that his sexiness was as much a part of him as his integrity. She didn't need to be feeling this softening toward him, this warmth that was spreading through her like melting butter. She needed to remember that her businesslike and brisk attitude had worked well for the past year and a half. She didn't need to change things now, or let him change things.

Becca knew exactly what she was going to do to keep that from happening. "It's time for you to rest," she said with a return to the briskness she'd worked so hard to perfect. "Jimmy's going to be home soon from Todd's and he'll expect you to play with him and you're in no condition to do that yet."

Clay's eyes narrowed and he opened his mouth as if he was going to comment on her no-nonsense attitude. That was the problem with nursing him; he knew her so well he knew when she was retreating into self-preservation. She lifted her chin, telling him she was the one in charge here.

Clay nodded and said, "This pillow's not quite right, though."

With a gusty sigh, Becca said, "We just did that, remember? You said it was fine now."

He gave her a puzzled look. "It must have scrunched down again while you were telling me what a model patient I am."

Becca fought the urge to thump him on the head with his water jug. Instead, she stepped forward. Leaning over the bed, she urged Clay to sit up with one hand while she tugged at the pillow with the other. When she touched him, she knew something was different. Less than five minutes ago, she had been able to do this with the efficiency of a professional nurse. Now she only seemed to notice the warmth of Clay's skin through his white T-shirt. She couldn't help it when her hand paused on his shoulder blade, her fingers stretching to press against the hardness of his muscles. She didn't want to realize that in spite of his injuries and his stay in the hospital, he felt to her touch the way he always had— strong and hard. He smelled the way he had always smelled; an indefinable combination of musky virility that she would never forget.

Becca stared at her hand, at her lightly tanned fingers resting millimeters from the reddened skin of his neck. She could see that he'd had a recent haircut. The skin at the edge of his hairline showed white. He was meticulous about his personal care; showering and shaving twice daily, and getting a haircut before he really needed one. He'd told her, in a rare moment of candor, that he'd once been placed in a foster home where the people's habits could only be described as slovenly. He swore it had turned him into a neatnik, but Becca suspected he would have been like that anyway. She'd appreciated knowing the reason behind it, but the small glimpse he'd given her into his past had only whetted her appetite for more.

With a start, Becca realized that Clay had gone very still, barely even seeming to breathe as her hand rested on his shoulder. Slowly, he turned his head and his dark green eyes sought her troubled blue ones. He was asking what she was doing, and she was darned if she could have told him. If she reacted like this to fluffing his pillows, how was she ever going to survive giving him a sponge bath?

Becca snatched her hand away and said, "Never mind the pillow." Her voice was raw and she took a breath, knowing that her face was red and flustered. "You need to rest and I...I need to...start, uh, dinner."

The corner of Clay's mouth quirked up. "It's two-thirty in the afternoon, Becca."

"I'm a slow cook," she snapped. Turning, she walked from the room, closing the door with a smart click and ignoring the chuckles coming from Clay.

CHAPTER FOUR

BECCA sank onto the sofa, pressed her elbows into her knees and dropped her face into her hands. She rubbed her fingertips against her forehead where she could feel a Clay-induced headache gathering like a thundercloud. This was not the first one she'd had this week and she suspected it wouldn't be the last one she would see before Clay Saunders was once more out of her life.

With a gusty sigh, she flopped against the back of the blue-checked sofa and propped her feet on the coffee table. Glumly, she considered the toes of her neatly polished loafers.

Clay had been in her house for six days now. As far as she could tell, he was improving rapidly. His headaches had all but disappeared. He spent less time sleeping. Instead, he was usually fully awake in order to give *her* headaches.

It wasn't that he was petulant or demanding. The difficult patient she had expected had never materialized. Instead, he was warm and cheerful, cooperative to a fault, and not excessively demanding.

Becca's eyes darkened as she studied the tips of her shoes. At least she didn't *think* he was excessively demanding. Whenever he needed something; a drink of water or juice, his pillows fluffed, or his wheelchair brought alongside the bed for a trip to the bathroom, he apologized for troubling her, and was grateful for her help. In fact, he said so repeatedly. She didn't mind giving him the help he needed, especially since he had shocked her by being a model patient. He didn't seem to mind waiting, either. If she was busy when he needed something, he was content to wait for her. In fact, he seemed happy to do it.

Since the day she had met him, she had found herself knocked breathless by his drive and determination. He'd always had plans and goals, though he hadn't always shared them with her. He'd had places to go and people to see, which was why he'd never been able to relax. Now he seemed satisfied to do what the doctor had said, which was to rest and recuperate. He didn't have a choice, of course, but he didn't seem to fret as she had expected him to. However, he did seem to need her frequent attention for some little thing or other. She was never able to get very far away from him.

As small as his demands were, he always needed something. Becca, who was determined to finish a needlepoint pillow she had been working on for weeks, finally carried her basket into his room and sat with him while he napped or read. If she left, he invariably called for her.

The real problem was that Becca spent so much time thinking about him, and puzzling over the changes in him which couldn't be explained by his bump on the head. She found herself more aware of him than she wanted to be. As expected, the sponge bath routine had been a nightmare. She had stumbled and bumbled through the first one and Clay had told her that if it made her so uncomfortable, he could handle it on his own. He'd been laughing at her the entire time, but she'd been glad to hand him the sponge and come back to carry away the basin of water when he was neatly tucked once again, into his pajamas.

Even without the sponge baths, she was so darned

aware of him and the awareness was physical as well as mental and emotional. Her reactions brought back more memories than she needed.

She knew she should welcome them as a way of gaining the closure she felt she had never achieved after the divorce. If she dealt with each emotion as it came, examined and categorized it, she was sure she could finally get over him. In fact, she had made a little mental list of the feelings she needed to conquer.

Too bad for her that he kept messing up her list.

Just as she was reminding herself that he had been emotionally distant during their marriage, he would turn to her with a warm, open smile that made her want to question and probe to know what he was feeling and thinking. When she recalled that he'd never wanted to own a home, to be tied down to one place, he would compliment her on the beauty and comfort of her home and run his hand over the hand-pieced quilt that Mary Jane had given her. The gesture made Becca's heart ache.

Why couldn't he have done that years ago? Why couldn't he have appreciated the things she'd tried to do to make their apartments into real homes? He'd never even seemed to notice until she'd pointed them out to him. She couldn't help feeling a little resentful of that.

He had always been a puzzle to her. When they first met, she had been so desperately in love with him, so wildly attracted, that she had tried to batter her way into his mind, to understand his thoughts, to know how much of his emotions were centered on her. She had finally given up on that and had long ago told herself that was best since they were no longer together. Now she felt those same ideas slipping through again. She wanted to know the reason behind the change in him. She knew it wasn't only because of the accident.

Becca was startled out of her thoughts by the slamming of the front door. She started and whipped around to see Jimmy and two of his friends troop into the house.

"Hi, Mom," he greeted her, dropping his book bag in the middle of the floor. His friends followed suit. "Got any cookies?"

Rolling her eyes, Becca stood to follow the boys into the kitchen where they filled up on cookies and milk and then talked about their plans for the afternoon. Jimmy had been disappointed over the canceled skiing trip, but he had adjusted to the idea and had something even better to talk about to his friends—his dad was home again and had a leg broken in *two* places. It was wrapped up in a big cast that all of Jimmy's friends could sign. When the boys finished their snacks, they trailed into the bedroom to visit Clay. Becca followed along because she couldn't get enough of seeing Clay being entertained by their son as he told and retold the story of the accident. It seemed that Jimmy's only regret was that *he* wasn't the one with the cast.

Becca had been amused by the way Jimmy carefully stuck to the facts of the story. She knew he was dying to embellish it with a tale about the two of them being caught in a rock slide or battling their way out of a flooded, abandoned mine. He stuck to the truth, though, because his dad was listening.

After the boys had duly admired the cast, signed their names, and bounced out again, Becca leaned against the doorjamb and said, "You've become the star attraction of the first grade. Better be careful, or Jimmy will want to take you in for sharing time."

"I thought that's what was happening now," Clay

answered as he examined the white plaster. "Do you know I've got sixteen names on this cast?"

Becca pushed away from the door frame and strolled into the room. "People will just think you have lots of friends."

"Who can't write in cursive," he added, examining one name with several letters turned backward. "Or spell."

Becca smiled. "Jimmy's proud of you. He likes having his father around." She shook her head in wonderment. "Do you have any idea how many children are from broken...." Her words faltered to a stop. *Theirs* was a broken home. She looked down at her hands. How could she have forgotten? Embarrassment washed through her and it was a moment before she could look up and meet Clay's eyes. She saw a hint of compassion there she hadn't expected. It was made all the more endearing because his face was still somewhat battered, though the bruising around his eye was fading.

"It's easy to forget sometimes, isn't it, Bec?" he asked quietly.

Her feeling of foolishness stiffened her pride, as well as her spine. "Of course not," she answered briskly. "Besides, his home won't be broken much longer."

Clay's sympathetic expression faded. He leaned against his pillow, crossed his arms over his chest, and said, "Oh, yes, the remarkable Barry."

"Barry will be good to Jimmy," Becca said defensively, still smarting from her careless words.

"A stepfather's not the same as a real father."

"A biased statement if ever there was one."

"But nevertheless true." Clay tilted his head and gave her an assessing look. "When do I get to meet this combination boss and fiancé of yours? I think I have a right to know what kind of man you're marrying, the type of guy who will be my son's stepfather."

She gave him an uncomfortable look. On the surface, the request seemed harmless enough. He was right. He did have a right to meet Barry and it would make things so much easier if the two of them could at least tolerate each other. Not that she was really worried. Barry was so easygoing, he could get along with just about anybody. Still, she didn't quite know what to say.

She folded her hands at her waist, and said in a cautious tone, "I'm a little surprised by this."

"Oh?" Clay asked innocently. "Why's that?"

"Because you blew your top when I told you I was marrying Barry."

"Your memory's a little faulty, Becca. I blew my top because you *didn't* tell me. Brittnie let it slip."

Becca's cheeks burned as she recalled her little attempt at subterfuge. "Well, okay, maybe you're right, but you were pretty angry."

"Mostly because you hadn't told Jimmy yet."

Becca was silent. She had no answer to that.

"So what's the problem with me meeting Barry? Afraid I'll try to throw a punch?" Clay tapped his cast. "Somebody would have to help me stand up first," he pointed out dryly.

Becca sighed. Maybe she *was* being too defensive. No doubt a reaction to the guilt she felt over the way she had tried to hide her engagement from him.

"Invite him over for dinner, Becca," Clay urged. "We could have a real family get-together."

She couldn't imagine the three of them sitting around the table, politely engaging in dinner conversation. She shook her head. "I really don't think that would be a good...."

"Scared, Becca?" He gave her a mocking look.

Her eyes widened. "Scared? Of what?"

His smile came then, spreading his lips slowly. He leaned his head back and gazed at her from beneath his lowered lids. "Of making comparisons between Barry..." His gaze shot up to meet hers. "..and me."

"Of course not!" Becca snapped. Her response was too quick and too sharp because he had skated so close to the truth. That was something she had studiously avoided doing. It wouldn't be fair to either man and she didn't want to carry such comparisons around in her head.

She decided to give his statement the broadest possible interpretation. "There's no comparison. You'll always be Jimmy's father, but Barry will be a good stepfather. He loves Jimmy."

"That's not what I mean."

Heat washed through her, only this time it wasn't caused by embarrassment. Irritation sharpened her voice. "You mean I'll be comparing you two as men?"

"It's possible."

"It's ridiculous. There's no comparison."

"*I* know that, Becca."

She caught his meaning immediately. "Why you arrogant son of a gun," she breathed.

"Maybe I am," he shrugged. "But don't forget, I know you."

"And what's that supposed to mean?"

"That I know what kind of man you like, what kind of man you need."

Her eyes flashed with irritation. "If you really knew that, we wouldn't be divorced right now."

"The divorce was a knee-jerk reaction on your part. You weren't willing to stay and work things out."

"You weren't willing to sit down and talk things over with me," she countered hotly.

"There's a time when talking doesn't do any good. Action is needed."

"Well, sir, I took action."

"Yeah," he said contemptuously. "Action that broke up our family."

"I did what was best for myself and for Jimmy."

"No," Clay said. "You did what you *thought* was best at the time. If you'd given it more thought, you wouldn't have gone through with it."

Furiously, Becca stared at him, at a loss for words. They always got to this point and got stuck. He wouldn't bend and she wouldn't back down. She got too angry too quickly and lost her perspective while he used logic and finesse to back her into a corner.

In the past, this had been the point where he would touch her, draw her to him, make passionate love to her, usually in silence, and she would be left with the frustrating feeling that they had once again failed to resolve the deepest problem between them—that she wanted to know and understand his heart and mind and he wouldn't let her in.

Divorce or no divorce, nothing had changed. She still didn't know him, understand him. The difference now was that she wasn't supposed to care.

She didn't really, she told herself. She simply wasn't accustomed to failure, which was what her marriage had been.

While these thoughts raced through her head, he leaned back and gave her a level stare.

"But this really isn't about me," he said. "It's about the man who supposedly will be stepfather to my son."

"There's no supposedly about it," she responded in

a tight voice. "Barry and I will be married and he will be a fine stepfather for Jimmy. We'll be very happy together," she added for good measure.

"Sounds like you're trying to convince yourself."

Her temper flared and she dropped her hands onto her hips. "I am not!"

"You're protesting too much."

"I'm not protesting," she sputtered. "I'm...I'm."

"Protesting."

She closed her mouth and glared at him.

"Becca, how will you know you're not making comparisons between us unless you invite him over and let the two of us meet?"

"I don't think you've heard a word I've said. Somehow that doesn't surprise me, though. You rarely listened to me when we were married."

The teasing light drained from his eyes to be replaced by a coolness she knew all too well. "I always listened to you, Rebecca, until you stopped making any sense."

Insulted, Becca straightened, answering him with a steady gaze. They were back to the divorce. Clay swore she had lost her senses when she'd told him she was leaving him and taking Jimmy. They had been at an impasse then, and they were still.

She decided to abandon the field of battle. "I'll call Barry and ask if he'd like to come to dinner tonight," she said. "His mother sent me her recipe for his favorite ham casserole. I've been wanting to try it out," she said by way of a payback as she turned to walk out.

"You were always good at cooking what your man liked to eat," Clay answered with genuine admiration that she found suspicious.

She glanced over her shoulder with a narrow-eyed look. "Yes, I was and *am*."

Clay leaned back and crossed his hands behind his head. "Old Barry is a lucky man," he said. "Ham casserole," he added in a voice that seemed to savor the very sound. "Delicious."

Disgruntled, Becca left the room and closed the door with a loud click. She didn't know what kind of game he was playing, but she didn't like it at all. Clay was strictly a meat-and-potatoes man. He wouldn't eat casseroles of any kind.

Her aquamarine eyes took on a decidedly vengeful glint. Maybe she would make banana cream pie for dessert. She had no idea if Barry liked it, but Clay loathed it and that was good enough reason for her to whip one up.

"I didn't know what to expect when I moved to the West," Barry commented as he sipped his coffee.

"You didn't?" Clay asked.

Becca watched carefully as Clay shifted in his chair. He cupped his hands around his coffee mug as if he was settling in for a long conversation. She had been on guard all evening, expecting Clay to make a biting comment to Barry, but he had been studiously polite since her fiancé had arrived. Releasing a little of her worry, she sat back, snuggling into her corner of the sofa, at the opposite end from Barry. She tucked her feet up, spread the skirt of her wine-red corduroy dress over them and took a sip of the pecan-flavored coffee she'd prepared. As she did so, she smiled ruefully to herself.

Barry had loved the dinner she'd prepared, praising it effusively, though he'd actually eaten very little. Beyond a few quietly appreciative comments, Clay hadn't said much, but he'd stunned her by eating two helpings of everything, including the banana cream pie. She felt petty for the little revenge she'd tried, but she was also feeling a bit confused because he'd actually seemed to *like* the casserole and the pie. Of course, she thought. Why not? He'd recently gone through some kind of personality change, and that must have included food preferences.

She glanced up as Clay lifted his coffee mug to take a sip. That hadn't changed. He still loved coffee and couldn't be induced to drink it from a cup and saucer under any circumstances. He liked big, thick mugs.

She glanced up just then and caught Clay gazing at something beside her. He looked up and raised an eyebrow as if asking a question. With a slight frown, Becca examined the sofa cushion between her and Barry. There was nothing there. Maybe he thought she shouldn't have her feet up on the sofa. Too bad, she thought, lifting her chin. It was her sofa. She could put her feet on it if she wanted. Her defiant look said as much.

Clay rolled his eyes at her as if she'd missed the point. Well, of course she'd missed the point, she thought huffily. She couldn't read his mind.

"No," Barry went on, oblivious of the byplay between the other two. "You see, I'd never been farther west than Kansas when I took the job here in Tarrant, but when my parents retired to Denver, I thought I should be close by so I started job-hunting. When I got the job with the Chamber of Commerce and moved here, I wasn't prepared for some of the customs in Tarrant."

"The, uh, customs?" Clay asked.

Becca saw Clay bite the corner of his lip and wondered if he was secretly amused at Barry. Her fiancé did sound a little like he had been suddenly transported to a remote corner of the earth instead of to one of the fifty states.

She set her cup down on the coffee table, turned to him, and said, "Oh, like what?"

"Like the sign in front of the public library that says No Guns Allowed."

Becca saw Clay's lips twitch, but his voice was serious as he answered, "I can see where that would be a surprise." After he spoke, he looked at Becca again, slid his gaze from her to Barry, then back again. He did this two or three times while Becca frowned at him, wondering if perhaps his mild concussion hadn't healed after all. Maybe she should call Dr. Kress. Clay seemed to be recovering nicely, but sometimes head injuries were tricky.

Clay met her look and shook his head slightly.

Barry seemed to be oblivious to Clay's little pantomime. He said, "In most eastern cities, you'd never see a sign in the library warning against guns."

"They're more likely to be on the subway," Clay commented.

Becca, who knew Barry loved New York City where he'd lived for several years, rushed to add, "My dad said that sign's been there since the forties. There was a beautiful young librarian who worked there and all the local cowboys liked to come in and flirt with her. They usually wore their firearms. I think the town council was afraid there might be a shootout over her, so they erected the sign. Dad knew all about it because the librarian was his aunt Katrina."

Clay chuckled. "Ah, Great-Aunt Katrina. She's had four husbands and is looking for number five. She's close to eighty...."

"Though she'll only admit to sixty," Becca added. They shared a smile over her quirky aunt.

"Your dad called her the divorce lawyer's best

friend," Clay recalled. "Because her lawyer always got a percentage of her alimony."

Becca snickered. "That's true."

Barry was quiet for a moment as he looked from one to the other of them. He took off his glasses and polished them on the napkin he'd spread across his knee. As he placed them back on his nose, he said, "I don't think I've met her."

Becca felt heat rise in her cheeks. "Uh, well, she's been in Arizona visiting her daughter for the winter, and we haven't had any family get-togethers lately...."

"At least not for three months," Clay added casually. "Pretty unusual for your family."

Darn him for remembering exactly how long she'd been dating Barry. She should have invited everyone over to meet him, but it seemed that the various family members had been too busy since Christmas for a party. Besides, Barry went to Denver most weekends to see his parents, then the accident had happened, so family gatherings were out of the question for a while.

She couldn't have one now, she thought, as she surveyed her lanky ex-husband stretched out in her best chair. How could she explain his presence to her nosy relatives? Even Aunt Katrina had possessed better sense than to have an ex-husband living with her while trying to marry someone else.

"Not very civilized to have a shootout over a woman," Clay said, returning the conversation to its starting place. He shifted in his chair again, seeming to settle more deeply into the cushions. He smiled slightly, sipped his coffee, and sighed with deep contentment.

Becca shifted uncomfortably. She would love to know what was going on in his mind.

"And they've never changed the sign?" Barry asked.

Becca shrugged when she heard the surprise in Barry's voice and said, "Nothing much changes in Tarrant." She took a sip of her coffee, but she couldn't help glancing at Clay over its rim. She had just echoed his reason for never wanting to live in a small town. Clay was a restless man. He liked change—a fact she had learned to her dismay when they'd been married only a few weeks.

"From what I hear, it might not hurt to post signs like that in New York," Clay observed. He met Becca's eyes and lifted one eyebrow to indicate he knew exactly what she was thinking.

Becca tensed for a second, reacting to his knowing look and still expecting to hear censure in Clay's voice directed at Barry. "But maybe they don't need to," he went on. "I hear the city's done an outstanding job of reducing crime."

"You're right. They have," Barry agreed. "Tarrant's a nice town." He looked up and gave Becca a warm smile. "I'm glad I moved here."

Becca smiled back, thinking what a pleasant, uncomplicated man he was. When she felt Clay's eyes on her, she gave him a cool look. She didn't know what he was playing at, but she wasn't going to let him rattle her.

The conversation continued amiably and Becca felt the knot she'd carried in her stomach all day begin to ease. Since Clay had brought up the idea of inviting Barry over earlier that day, she had been expecting the worst, but this was turning out very well—at least now that Clay seemed to have settled down.

In order to keep Jimmy occupied and happy, she had suggested that he invite a friend to sleep over. The two boys had eaten dinner and gone off to Jimmy's room to play, leaving the adults to make stiff conversation and small talk.

Only it hadn't been stiff. While he hadn't actually been playing the part of host because he was a guest in her home, too, Clay had gone out of his way to draw Barry out, get him to talk about himself. She would like to think it was because Clay wanted to know as much as possible about this man who was going to be step-father to his son, but she had the feeling there was more to Clay's interest. She couldn't quite shake the feeling that Clay was looking for a reason to dislike Barry. She already knew he wanted to point up the differences between himself and Barry and force her into unwanted comparisons.

Becca's uncertainty kept her in a state of nervous expectation all evening, but the conversation flowed easily between the two men with occasional comments from her. The upcoming wedding wasn't discussed; they stuck to neutral topics, but Becca took the pleasantries as a hopeful sign.

Clay had even insisted on sitting in the club chair so she and Barry could share the sofa. Becca sat up suddenly, and her feet hit the floor.

Barry stopped in midsentence and turned to her. "Something wrong, Rebecca?"

Her face filled with embarrassment. "No. No, it's just that…my foot went to sleep." She shook it experimentally. "It's fine now."

She gave Clay a peeved look. That's what all that eye-shifting had been about. He was silently asking why she wasn't sitting close to Barry, snuggled with him at one end of the couch the way she and Clay had always done when they were first together.

He smiled benignly, while she stood and moved closer

to Barry, who gave her a perplexed look when she plopped down on the center cushion and lifted a brow at Clay as if to say, "See there?"

When she stood, Barry's impeccable manners had him shooting to his feet. He stood awkwardly for a few seconds, then his gaze darted to Clay as if asking the other man's permission to sit close to her. Becca reached up and grabbed his hand to tug him down. Barry tilted down awkwardly beside her, nearly dropping his cup and saucer. Clay's grin looked as if he was bestowing a blessing on them. Becca couldn't help the tightening of her lips as she realized she had just fallen into the trap he'd set.

She was quiet for the rest of the evening, listening to the conversation between the two men, and found herself making comparisons as Clay had suggested she would. She realized quickly that Clay was forceful and direct as always and Barry was a peacemaker. It was one of the things that made him good at his job, and made him so easy to be with. As far as she was concerned, that was definitely a point is his favor.

After a while, Clay said he was tired. Becca thought that sounded a little suspicious because he seemed quite robust to her. When she said as much, he treated her to a wan smile.

"Oh, but I am, Becca. I'm not used to this much excitement."

Her eyes widened. It was quite a statement from a man who'd once been treed by a bear while working in Alaska.

Barry started to his feet again. "Can I help you get to bed?" he offered.

The look Clay shot him could have stopped a rogue elephant, but he smoothed it over and said, "Uh, no thanks."

Standing, Becca held the wheelchair while Clay lifted himself into it, then she pushed him into his room. She wasn't even sure why she was there. As usual, Clay pushed himself to regain his independence and he needed her less and less to help him prepare for bed.

Once he was settled, he lay against the pillows, stacked his hands beneath his head and studied her with a look she couldn't quite read, though it seemed to border on satisfaction.

"I know what you're thinking," she said accusingly, clapping her hands onto her hips.

"Oh, what's that?" he asked with an innocent widening of his green eyes.

"You're thinking that if I truly loved Barry, I would have been sitting close to him on the couch."

"You mean close like you and I always did, since we couldn't keep our hands off each other?"

"That's right," she said with a decisive nod, then paused. Maybe that wasn't exactly what she meant.

"Far be it from me to tell you how to treat your fiancé, Becca. You're a woman who knows her own mind, but, um, maybe you should let your body in on what you're thinking. It doesn't seem to know you're actually supposed to like this guy."

Fury shot through her. "Oh, you...pompous...know-it-all...."

"Uh, uh, uh," he said, wagging a finger at her. "Be careful what you say. Remember, I'm the father of your son."

"Too bad there's nothing I can do about that," she fumed. "For your information, Barry and I are mature adults. We don't need to...to paw each other like a couple of teenagers, or...."

"Or like most engaged couples, or like you and I did

when we first met, and for several years after that?''
Clay asked in a dry tone.

Becca opened her mouth to zing him with a sharp
retort, but this was a pointless discussion. She knew it
would definitely not be in her best interest to say, ''Oh,
yeah, well maybe I don't feel about Barry the way I felt
about you!'' No matter how she meant it, that statement
could never be made to come out right.

''Another thing I've wondered about,'' Clay went on.
''Is why you don't have an engagement ring? Can't af-
ford one?''

Becca couldn't resist the urge to look down at her bare
hand. She had finally lost the pale shadow left when
she'd removed her wedding band. ''We simply decided
to save our money for a nice honeymoon trip.'' Also,
she'd known that a new diamond would have brought
many questions from Jimmy that she wasn't prepared to
answer, but she certainly wasn't going to tell Clay *that!*

She changed the subject. ''At least you should be
grateful that I'm getting Jimmy a good stepfather.''

''If that's why you're planning to marry him, I guess
you could do worse.'' Clay rubbed his chin thoughtfully.
''He seems like a nice guy.''

Still she blinked at him suspiciously and tried to find
an insult hidden in his words. ''I told you he was. He's
good to Jimmy, but he's not going to try to take your
place in Jimmy's life.''

Clay lifted an eyebrow at her. ''I can see that.''

''Well, well, good,'' she answered with a nod, surprised by his quick agreement.

''Yes, sir,'' he said quietly, looking up at the ceiling.
''I can see I have nothing to worry about at all.''

She stared, her irritation giving way to a trickle of
forgiveness toward him, but her smile remained stiff.

"I'm so glad you see it that way. I have to admit that from your first reaction, I thought you'd be much more opposed to my remarriage."

Clay's gaze came back to her for a long look. "I'm not opposed to it at all," he said. "I think remarriage is the ideal thing for you."

She was so surprised, it was a minute before she could catch her breath. "Why, Clay...I don't know what to say...I...."

"Just say good-night, Becca," he said, and yawned. "And switch off the light as you leave."

Becca did as he asked, turning one last time to say, "Clay, I appreciate your change in attitude."

"No problem, Bec," he answered from the darkness. "I'm glad to know I have nothing to worry about."

Becca paused, still not quite able to reconcile his change of heart with his pointed references to the distance she'd kept from Barry. This probably wasn't the time to pursue it, though, so she went out and closed the door. She was so relieved at his change of heart that she convinced herself it wasn't quiet amusement she'd heard in his voice.

Back in the living room, she found Barry standing by the door with his coat on.

"Oh, you don't have to go yet, do you?" she asked, glancing at the clock. "It's still early."

"I've got to go," he said, reaching out to take her hands. "I've got the Rotary Club breakfast in the morning and they've asked me to make a little speech." He leaned over to give her a kiss on the cheek.

Becca looked up suddenly, longing for him to take her in his arms and kiss her as passionately as Clay always had, then immediately wished she hadn't let the thought form. Barry was a reserved man and he certainly would never do such a thing knowing Clay was in the house.

"Rebecca," Barry said slowly. "How long does it take for a married couple to develop those private little jokes about families and relationships like you and Clay have?"

Dismayed, Becca said, "I...I don't know. Not long, I guess."

"You still seem very...connected to him."

"We lived together as husband and wife for five years and we've been divorced for less than one."

Barry pulled his gloves from his coat pocket and tugged them on. "And it takes time, to change, to get over him." He gazed down the hallway. "Maybe this wasn't such a good idea, after all."

"Him staying here, you mean? You're probably right, but I didn't have much choice." She really didn't know what else to say so she said nothing.

Barry looked back at her, his kind brown eyes full of understanding. "I know this isn't easy for you, either. Just remember, you're trying to put him behind you."

She nodded, gave him a hug, and watched as he left. After closing the door, she wandered around the living room, picking up their coffee things and straightening the cushions and pillows. Barry was right, of course. Clay was in her past. Too bad he didn't seem content to stay there.

CHAPTER FIVE

FOR the next two days, Becca went around the house with the uneasy feeling that she didn't quite know what was going to happen next. True, Clay actually appeared to like her future husband, and Barry had seemed relieved to meet Clay, in spite of Barry's realization that she was still very connected to Clay. She had to admit it was true.

As for Jimmy, he was thrilled to have his dad with them. Of course, the boy didn't seem to quite understand that it was only temporary, but she would deal with that when the time came. She had enough to deal with right now.

Clay had begun showing his true colors as a patient—he was beginning to chafe at the confines of her small house and was growing bored with television which he'd never liked much, anyway. He wasn't interested in reading the type of fiction she liked. She knew she was going to have to make a trip to the public library to find him something to read.

A book about rocks, she thought grumpily, as she stared at him across the top of the chessboard she'd set up on a small table by his bed. Rocks to match the ones in his head.

Joey Emerson had come over several times, no doubt at his father's prompting, to ask if he could help out. Becca had assigned him to play chess with Clay. He'd promptly lost the match, fled the house, and not returned. Poor kid, she thought in sympathy. She knew why now.

Clay was too good at the game and didn't waste any time in defeating his opponent.

The chess set had been her father's. Mary Jane had given it to her for Jimmy, who she hoped would treasure it someday. Right now Becca was using it to keep Clay entertained, though she had to admit it didn't seem to be working very well.

She sighed as he checkmated her once again. She wasn't good at chess while he was a strategist's dream. He wasn't a patient man, yet he could spend an hour studying a chessboard, figuring every angle and possible move. She made foolish moves in hopes of finishing the game quickly so she could go do something she actually enjoyed.

This was another of the differences between them— he was good at everything he tried, while she rarely tried anything she didn't already know she was good at.

"Playing chess with you isn't much of a challenge, Becca," Clay complained in a mild tone.

"That's not news to either one of us," she answered as she began putting away the pieces with quiet efficiency, secretly thrilled to be finished with the game. If she hurried, she would have time to work in her small garden before she started dinner preparations. She had begun turning the soil over in readiness for the flowers she hoped to plant in the next few weeks and she was eager to finish the job. "Besides," she said absently as she fit the last piece into its slot. "I'm not here to provide you with a challenge."

Clay's hand shot out to encircle her wrist. She squeaked in surprise and her gaze flew to meet his.

His dark eyes, which had been calculating a chess move only moments ago, now glittered at her.

"Oh, but you do provide a challenge, Becca. You always have."

Her mouth went dry as she stared at him. They weren't talking about chess now.

She stared down at his hand; his long, tanned fingers against her pale skin. He worked with his hands, so they were calloused, but never rough. He kept them scrupulously clean, a fact she had always appreciated when he had touched her like this.

Reluctantly, Becca raised her eyes to meet his. "Clay...."

"In fact, you were always a challenge to me, Becca." His lips quirked, belying the seriousness in his eyes. "Though not in chess," he said.

The intensity in his eyes finally helped her locate her voice. She cleared her throat briskly. "Clay, I don't know what you're thinking, but you're only...only my patient. The reason you're here is to recover from the wreck...."

"Now don't get prickly," he soothed, the timbre of his voice dropping. "My thoughts are so pure, they could be in a G-rated movie."

"I'll bet," she muttered.

"See there, Becca. There you go again, doubting me."

"I've had lots of practice," she answered. "I'm quite good at it."

"Did it ever occur to you that most of the things you doubted about me, most of the things you worried about, were never really based in reality?"

Becca slipped the lid onto the box of chess pieces. Her hands gripped the corners. "I would ask what on earth you mean, but I really don't want to know."

Clay loosely clasped her wrist. Becca tried to pull

away. She had always responded to the warmth and vitality of his touch and that hadn't changed. But now, she didn't *want* this. Clay tightened his grip. "I mean that you built things up in your mind, worried over things that we could have worked out."

She shook her head emphatically. "No, I didn't. I..."

"Yes, you did, and it started when your dad died. That's when you changed, Becca."

She gaped at him. "When *I* changed?"

"That's right. Then you miscarried and things just got worse."

The pain of her memories from that time washed over her again, coupled with the fresh pain of his accusations. "Clay, things hadn't been working between us for a long time before that."

"Maybe so," he conceded. "But you suddenly expected me to be something I'd never been before."

"You mean stable, willing to stay in one place longer than six months?" she asked hotly.

"I'm a mining engineer, Becca. I've got to go where the jobs are."

"There are engineering jobs in mining that last for years," she answered in frustration. "More than years. Careers."

"True, but they're not in my field."

"And you wouldn't change fields."

"I like what I do," he pointed out. "I like being on the move. You didn't seem to mind when we met, when we married."

"I didn't know what was involved in your job."

"Even when you knew, it wasn't a problem at first," he shot back.

"But things changed." Her eyes were troubled, her

face full of pain. She shook her head. "You're right. I *did* change, but you didn't."

"You're wrong there, Becca. I changed, too, but not in the way you wanted me to."

"Clay," she said wearily as she twisted her hand, trying to pull from his grasp. "We've had this discussion before and nothing's ever been resolved."

"That's because we spent too much time talking," he said, his voice dropping. "It was never our best way of communicating."

With one hand, he shoved the box of chess pieces aside and with the other, he pulled her toward him. He maneuvered her so that she fell, half-reclining against him, held firmly against his right side.

Panic beat at her, as Becca frantically tried to decide how to handle this. She wouldn't resist, she decided instantly. That only challenged him. He loved a challenge.

Instead, she looked at him steadily, her direct gaze telling him she knew what he intended and she wouldn't be a willing participant.

She knew he got the message because his lips quirked knowingly. He slipped his hands up her arms, then around her waist. With a steady motion, he drew her to him and his mouth claimed hers.

Oh, no, she thought when his familiar, sensuous warmth stole through her. This was like the first kiss he'd ever given her. They'd met, gone out, and had their first kiss all in one day. That kiss had changed her life. They'd been standing in the foyer of her small apartment over on Mallen Street with wisps of October cold curling beneath the door. She remembered everything about it—the frigid tile under her bare feet, the heat of his arms enfolding her. When Clay had held her, she had known instantly that things would never be the same for her, that this man would change her life forever.

She'd been younger, much more vulnerable then. She was stronger now. She could hold out, she told herself, until he realized his forcefulness wasn't going to get a response from her.

But in spite of the way he'd started out, it wasn't forcefulness he employed. It was finesse. Clay's lips possessed hers lightly, cautiously, as if he hadn't kissed her a thousand times before, as if their kisses didn't always lead to a conflagration of passion. His mouth touched, moved away, came back, settled.

The touch was light enough so that she could have pulled away any second. She knew that, she felt it in the way his lips moved over hers, tantalizing her, but not fulfilling the ache that was growing inside her. She felt it in the way his hands held her; palms firmly against her, but his fingers splayed. She could have slipped away from him effortlessly, but something in her chose not to.

Becca's eyelids, which she'd been determined to keep open, fluttered and somehow drifted shut. It meant nothing, she told herself. She would be better able to concentrate on resisting him. But her jaw trembled and they both knew it was an acceptance.

When his arms came up and around her, when he leaned back and drew her across his chest, she didn't resist. In fact, she murmured deep in her throat, a quiet little cry of need, and followed where he led. She had been holding her hands clenched into fists, but now they opened, flexed on the muscles of his arms, then ran up his shoulders.

Clay pulled away briefly. "Do you remember this, Becca? Do you remember that it was always like this with us?"

She blinked at him, trying to fight her way out of the sensual fog. "No, I...." she began, but he didn't give her time to finish. He kissed her again, this time abandoning the finesse to bring his forceful will to bear.

Becca wanted to fight, she knew she should, but she gave up the struggle with hardly a moment's resistance. The need between them was much stronger than she'd let herself expect.

Suddenly, Clay wrapped his hands around her upper arms and drew her away. "Becca, listen."

"What?" She blinked owlishly at him. She wanted to sink back into the lovely oblivion he had created. "No, I..."

Regret washed over his face as he ran a finger down her flushed cheek. "The doorbell, Becca. Someone's at the door."

Becca finally came to herself. She looked into his eyes, which were deep green with amusement and satisfaction.

She heard the doorbell peal. She didn't know how many times it had rung already. Scrambling up, she stumbled away from him. "You had no right to do that," she insisted breathlessly.

He smiled. "That's a little hard to accept from you when your lips are still swollen from being kissed."

She pushed her hair back from her face, too distraught to care that her hands were trembling. "You had no *right!* We're divorced."

Clay leaned back, propped his hands behind his head. "Like I said, it's easy to forget, isn't it?"

Cursing herself for fleeing from him, for letting him have the last word—again—Becca turned and rushed through her house to answer the door. She grasped the knob and flung it open, then stood and stared stupidly at her sister Brittnie, and at her own good friend, Lauren Wilberson.

"Becca?" Brittnie asked cautiously, studying her sister's face. "Are you all right?"

Becca nodded, although her eyes were full of distress. She might as well have a big neon sign over her head. One that said, Just Been Kissed Breathless By Ex-husband.

"If this is a bad time, we can come back," Lauren offered. She was a bright, funny woman who stood nearly six feet tall and had a booming, self-confident laugh. Now, though, she looked as if she thought Becca might faint and she needed to be prepared to catch her.

Becca finally gathered her wits. "No, no, this is fine," she said, stepping back and sweeping out her hand to invite them in. "Why did you say you dropped by?"

Brittnie and Lauren exchanged a look. "To plan your bridal shower, remember?"

Embarrassment washed over her. "Oh, of course. Uh, yes." She ran her palms down her thighs, dampening the front of the long, pink cotton sweater she wore over her navy blue slacks. Glancing down, she saw that it was wrinkled where it hadn't been wrinkled a little while ago.

In despair, she couldn't decide what made her more angry—Clay's assumption that he could get her to respond in the same old way, or herself for proving him right.

She couldn't think about that now. The others were staring at her in alarm. She had to gather her wits. Too bad she hadn't made that decision ten minutes ago. She should have fought Clay and not been concerned about the challenge she presented him.

"Come in," Becca said again.

"Sis, we *are* in," Brittnie pointed out.

"Oh, of course." Becca shut the door. "Well, then, sit down. I'll go and...and...make some coffee." She blurted out the last phrase as if she'd been struck with divine inspiration. Leaving her gaping guests, she whipped around and scurried into the kitchen.

As she shakily gathered coffee filters and the pecan-flavored coffee Brittnie liked, Becca frantically wondered how she'd reached this point. How had she let things get so far out of hand that she would be stupid enough to fall—once again—for Clay's sexy attractiveness? She was the world's greatest expert on what a mistake that was, and yet she had walked right back into it with her eyes wide open.

Eyes open and mind switched off, she concluded as she watched the coffee drip into the pot and breathed in the wonderful scent as it filled the kitchen. She had to decide how she was going to handle this before she faced Clay again.

After a moment's agonized thought, she decided she would simply act as if nothing had happened. She took a few quick, deep breaths and reached for calmness. She could do this, she thought with satisfaction. All she had to do was keep her wits about her, the same wits that had deserted her in the bedroom.

Confidently, she strode from the room, tray in hand, smiling as she heard Lauren's rich, deep chuckle. Her smile froze as her gaze swept the room and she saw Clay seated comfortably in her best easy chair, his casted leg resting on the matching hassock. The wheelchair was nowhere in evidence so she assumed he'd hopped on one foot from his room to the living room to join the guests. He hadn't even used the crutches she'd just picked up at the hospital.

At one time, she would have been surprised that he'd made the effort. Though not rude, Clay hadn't really been outgoing with her friends and family. Now here he was, the center of attention. Crossly, Becca decided she was going to ask Frank Kress if he had given Clay a personality transplant when he'd treated his head injury and set his broken leg.

With a grim look, Becca continued into the room. "Are you going to be joining us, Clay?" she asked in an unwelcoming voice.

"I already have," he answered, his sharp green eyes taking in the high color in her cheeks and the fury in her eyes. "If you don't mind."

Becca gave him a frosty smile, then her gaze touched on the faces of her guests who stared, breathless at the drama being played out before them. "Not at all. I'll get another coffee cup."

"I'll get it," Brittnie offered, scrambling to her feet. She dashed away and was back in an instant with a thick blue mug. She handed it to Becca who took it, splashed coffee into it, and all but shoved it into Clay's waiting hands.

He grinned. "Thanks, Bec."

Fuming, she poured for her guests and herself, then forced herself to sit back rather than perch tensely on the edge of her chair. "Well," she said. "What do we need to talk about?"

Lauren gave her an ironic smile and said, "The location, for one thing. Remember, we were going to have it at my house? Well, Steve and I are having a new roof put on the house. The roofers were supposed to start next month, but they had a cancellation, so they're going to start next week. The place will be torn up right when we've planned the shower."

Becca said, "Don't worry about it. It's not necessary to have a shower for me, anyway. Barry and I have everything we need, and...."

"We were thinking of a lingerie shower," Brittnie supplied, sipping her coffee and giving her older sister an expectant look over the rim of the cup.

"Oh," Becca said, and for some reason her gaze shot to Clay. He raised an appreciative brow at her.

"We can't have the shower at my place," Brittnie went on. "It's too small and I don't think it would be fair to ask Mom if we can have it at the ranch. She's so busy right now."

"That's true," Becca answered. "Well, it's not that important that I have a shower at all...."

Clay broke in. "Why not have it here?"

Brittnie and Lauren turned to look at him with interest. Becca burst into speech. "No. We can't do that."

"I don't see why not."

"Because, Mr. Manners, the shower is for me," she answered sardonically. "It would be crass to have it at my home."

"I disagree," he said, setting his mug down. "All these people are your friends and relatives, aren't they?"

"Yes, of course, but...."

"Then they'd understand." He gave her a soulful look that had her mouth dropping open, then he turned to look at the other women in the same way. "Besides, do you really think I should be left alone all evening?"

Lauren blinked in surprise, obviously taken aback by his question and the slight worry that creased his forehead. Becca gave her friend an irritated look. Lauren's heart was as soft as melting marshmallows.

"Oh, well, maybe he's right," Lauren said, and Brittnie broke in, "What if he needed something?"

Becca stared at her sister. "Well, obviously, he could get it for himself."

"What if I have a relapse?" Clay asked, his pitiful expression begging for sympathy.

"What if I break your other...?"

"Uh, uh, uh," he interrupted, wagging his finger at her. "First rule of being a good nurse is to never threaten the patient with bodily harm."

Brittnie and Lauren laughed at the thunderous expression on Becca's face.

"Seriously, Becca," Brittnie said. "Clay's right. Everyone would understand if we had the shower here. You have to admit that few people in Tarrant would even know that's not proper etiquette, much less object to it."

Becca started to protest again, but the three of them wore her down. Eventually it was agreed that the lingerie shower would be held a week later at Rebecca's house. The wedding date hadn't actually been set yet, but Brittnie had polled all of their friends and relatives and discovered that the coming week offered the best opportunity for most of them to get together.

When the arrangements were made, the guests finished their coffee and left. Becca closed the door behind them, then turned and fixed her ex-husband with a look that could have frozen a hot water geyser.

"You're a manipulative son of a...."

"Uh, uh, uh. Watch your language," he said, shaking his finger at her. "You never know when Jimmy might walk in."

Becca glanced at the clock. "He won't be home for fifteen minutes."

Clay lifted his arms and clasped them behind his head.

"Gives you just enough time to tear a strip off of me, hmm?"

"If necessary. Clay, you had no right to interfere, to manipulate us the way you did."

"You're the only one objecting," he pointed out.

"Well, you somehow managed to dazzle Brittnie and Lauren into agreeing with you."

Clay grinned and sat forward. "You know, honey, I think you just gave me a compliment."

"It wasn't intentional, believe me."

With a long-suffering sigh, Clay said, "When we were married you used to complain that I was unbending, that I wasn't willing to accommodate you or your family, that I wouldn't compromise. I was only trying to help think of a reasonable solution to your dilemma."

"It wasn't a dilemma and we could have solved it without your interference," Becca answered hotly, then stopped, realizing she was beginning to sound strident. She snapped her mouth shut, knowing she'd lost the argument, anyway. Turning, she said, "I've got work to do in the kitchen."

"Aren't you going to help me back to bed?" he asked wistfully.

"You got out of it on your own," she replied coolly. "You can get back into it on your own."

"Funny, I never knew you had such a heartless streak," Clay said as he pulled himself out of the chair and balanced on his good leg.

"It's the new me," she answered, sailing into the kitchen. She heard him making his way down the hall as she pulled out her recipe box and began assembling the ingredients for Jimmy's favorite peanut butter cookies.

As she whipped together shortening and peanut butter

and beat in the brown sugar, her mind worked furiously. She felt that since the moment of Clay's accident, she had been playing catch-up. He had awakened in the hospital a different man than the one she knew, but she had continued to react to him as if he was the old Clay.

The old Clay. Becca's hand slowed, then stopped, and she stared down at the golden-brown mass sticking to her wooden spoon. The true problem in her dealings with Clay was in her reactions to him. Even though she suspected that the man she knew lurked somewhere beneath the surface of this amiable, flirtatious stranger, she needed to change her method of dealing with him. So far, all she'd done was react to the outrageous things he said and did, like kissing her when he knew it wasn't what she wanted. Well, even if she had responded to him, she *hadn't* wanted to. He'd taken her by surprise.

Yup, she definitely had to change the way things were with them. She had to regain control. After all, this was her house and she had been the one to invite him here for his recuperation. She was in charge and she had to show it.

But how?

Becca thought it over as she finished mixing the cookies, working through the problem. As she placed a batch in the oven to bake, the front door slammed and Jimmy thundered into the house, heading straight for his dad's bedroom.

Jimmy was the other problem she needed to tackle in a forthright manner. Afraid of upsetting him, she hadn't been forceful enough in explaining that Clay's stay with them was only temporary. That had to change. He liked Barry and would accept him as a stepfather, but right now, her son seemed to think that matters were going to return to the way they'd been before she and Clay divorced. That wasn't going to happen, but it would take a while for Jimmy to understand that.

In the meantime, *she* was the one who had to change. As she watched the cookies baking, she formed a plan.

"Clay, I think you need a change of scenery," Becca said breezily as she swept into his room a short time later.

"Kicking me out, are you?" he asked, laying aside the book he'd been reading to Jimmy.

Their son looked up anxiously and Becca quickly said, "No. I mean we're going for a drive. We both need to get out of the house and it's a nice day. I made cookies to take along, and some hot chocolate. We'll go somewhere and have a picnic."

Jimmy bounced onto his knees. "You mean a snacknic," he corrected excitedly. "I'll go get my stuff." He scrambled from the bed and dashed from the room.

"He has to take 'stuff' on a picnic?" Clay asked.

"He takes 'stuff' everywhere," Becca said with a sigh. "You wouldn't believe the amount of junk he hauls around with him in that old backpack you gave him, but his teacher tells me that all little boys do that." Briskly, she turned to leave the room.

"They do?" Clay asked, his gaze drifting to the doorway where their son had disappeared. "I remember doing that, but I thought it was because...."

She paused, looking back at him. "Because what, Clay?"

His green eyes held a faraway expression that made Becca's breath catch. She hoped he would go on. Even though they'd been married for over five years, he had rarely talked about his childhood. It had been a source of conflict between them, but one they'd never discussed, a part of the silent war they'd waged with her trying to find out what went on inside him, and him equally determined to keep her from doing so.

Maybe this new Clay would tell her, though. Becca felt an ache just below her breastbone and pressed her hand against it.

After a moment, Clay went on. "Because I never knew if my things would be there when I got back."

"You moved a lot," she said. At least she knew that much, and that his mother had finally abandoned him to the foster care system when he was nine. She imagined him, a little boy who looked exactly like Jimmy, though not nearly so well cared for, left alone and frightened, to fend for himself. Somehow it clouded her whole picture of the self-sufficient man he'd become.

She opened her mouth to say how sorry she was, but his eyes cleared and he put up his hand as if to ward off her sympathy.

"We're going in your car, I assume," Clay said with a look that challenged her to dare returning to the subject he wanted to ignore.

Ah, she thought. Here was the old Clay. Not gone, after all, just dormant for a while. She didn't know why she felt so disappointed. After all, they were divorced. If he wanted to keep things hidden from her, it didn't matter anymore. She cleared her throat. "No, we're not taking my car. Since your Explorer's been fixed, I'll drive that."

Clay's eyes narrowed. "You don't like driving the Explorer."

"I've never *tried* driving the Explorer. What I didn't like driving was that three-quarter-ton pickup you used to have. It was as big as a tank."

Clay grinned reminiscently and Becca marveled at how quickly he could switch off the deep emotion he'd been feeling just moments before.

He said, "As I remember, it had a big front seat. It was just perfect for certain things."

They'd made love on that seat one night, Becca recalled. Even though she could feel a flush climbing her cheeks, she lifted her chin. "As *I* remember, you pulled a muscle in your back and couldn't stand up straight for a week."

"Ah, but it was worth it."

She gave him a flippant smile. "Do you want to be left alone to stroll down memory lane, or are you coming with us?"

"I'm coming," he answered with a grin. "Are you going to help me get ready?"

She folded her hands at her waist and tilted her head to the side. "Why, no, I'm not, as a matter of fact. You seem to be managing just fine on your own today. I will carry your crutches for you, though," she said, grabbing them from the corner where they'd been propped beside the wheelchair. "At least I'm assuming you're well enough to use these instead of the wheelchair."

He waggled his eyebrows at her. "Honey, I'm well enough for a lot of things."

"Good," she said, striding out the door. "I'll make you a list of household chores."

She heard Clay make a comment about "a sassy woman" and she smiled, satisfied that she was beginning to gain control of the situation.

Within ten minutes, they were loaded into the car with her driving and Clay in the seat beside her. They'd pushed it all the way back to accommodate his cast and Jimmy was strapped safely into the back seat.

Becca's plans for a "snacknic" went awry because once Clay and Jimmy caught a whiff of the freshly baked cookies, they dug into the bag and helped themselves, munching happily as she backed out of the driveway.

"Where shall we go?" she asked.

"The Lucy Belle," Jimmy shouted, nearly choking himself on a mouthful of cookie. "I wanna show Dad."

"The Lucy Belle?" Clay asked. "The old silver mine?"

"Yeah," Jimmy answered. "I know just how to get there, Mom. I'll tell you."

Clay gave her a quick glance as she followed Jimmy's directions and turned the Explorer toward the dirt road that led up to the mine. It was nearly two miles to the place and almost all of it was straight up.

As she drove, Jimmy chatted incessantly about the wonders of the mine. "You know, people could live in a mine if they didn't have a house. It would be just like camping out."

"It wouldn't be very comfortable, son." Clay laughed and glanced over at Becca who shared a warm smile with him. If they'd had more moments like this in their marriage, they probably wouldn't be divorced now.

"It would be okay if you had food and water and a flashlight and stuff," Jimmy concluded, and Clay couldn't change his mind.

When they reached the turnoff and could see the yawning mouth of the mine entrance, she pulled over and stopped the Explorer. Jimmy immediately unbuckled his seat belt and grabbed his backpack which contained the things he referred to as his "mining gear," a small pickax that Barry had bought for him, a flashlight, and some bottles of water. Chattering excitedly, he reached for the door handle, but Clay twisted around and stopped him. "You have to wait for us, son. You're not going near that entrance alone."

Jimmy gave Clay one of those looks that little boys reserve for adults who aren't very bright. "Dad, I've been here before. I know where I'm going."

"You'll wait for us," Clay repeated sternly.

With a miffed look, Jimmy subsided and waited impatiently while Becca helped Clay from the Explorer. Their progress over the rough ground was slow, but eventually they reached the opening of the mine. Jimmy immediately plunked his backpack onto the ground and began assembling his gear, seemingly not intimidated by the cavelike entrance. It rose before them, wide and dark. The thick timbers, as big around as a good-size man, looked sturdy in the afternoon light, as if they'd stood for a hundred years and could stand for a hundred more. In spite of that, Clay frowned at them.

"I wish you and your boyfriend had never brought him here," he grumbled as he lowered himself onto a large boulder and rested his hands on the crossbraces of his crutches.

She didn't remind him that Barry was far more than a boyfriend, but focused, instead, on his true concern. "Clay, this whole area is dotted with abandoned mines. If we hadn't brought Jimmy here he would have found it, or another one, on his own. Considering how crazy he is about rocks and minerals, he would have wanted to see one of the mines eventually. Don't you think it's better that he be here with supervision?"

"I think he could have waited until he'd learned a few survival techniques before coming up here. Look at that entrance," he said in disgust. "It's not even posted with warning signs."

"There used to be some," Becca answered, glancing

around. "They must have gotten knocked down. When I was in high school this was a lover's lane and lots of kids came up here for drinking parties, just like they've done at most of the old mines around here for years. I guess it's fallen out of favor," she added, waving her hand. "Not many beer cans around."

Clay's green eyes filled with interest. "Oh, yeah, who'd you come up here with?"

Becca gave him a dry look, but she wished she hadn't mentioned it. "No one."

"No wild boyfriend bringing you up here and trying to talk you out of your...." He glanced at their son. "Innocence?"

"Clay, are you kidding? You knew my dad. If he'd even *thought* I was parked up here, or anywhere else, with a boy, he would have come after me and dragged me home."

Clay gave her a speculative look. "Yeah, I can see Hal doing that. I'll probably do the same thing when we have a daughter."

CHAPTER SIX

"I'M READY!" Jimmy shouted.

Stunned by what Clay had said about a daughter, Becca barely heard the boy. "Clay," she began.

He gave a quick shrug. "Slip of the tongue," he answered smoothly. "I meant when *I* have a daughter."

While he turned to Jimmy, who was waiting expectantly for their attention, Becca stared at Clay, stricken. The two babies she had miscarried had both been girls. Except to offer sympathy, and to hold her when she'd needed him to, Clay hadn't said much about his feelings on the miscarriages. She had thought it hadn't affected him deeply. Something in his tone just now, though, had told her he'd wanted a daughter as much as she had. Was it possible that he'd been as hurt as she was, but had hidden it in his characteristic way?

Just this afternoon he'd said her father's death, and then the miscarriages had been the point when she had changed. He was probably right because that's when she had begun to realize that things were hopeless between them. Before that, she had stumbled along in a fool's paradise—and she had never known he'd truly wanted a daughter.

Becca was stunned by the news and deeply troubled by the swell of jealousy she felt at the idea that he might have a daughter with someone else.

Dazed, she put the thought aside because it was too disturbing to face right now and looked at Jimmy. Clay was chuckling softly.

Jimmy had tied lengths of rope onto his water bottles and slung them across his chest, pushed his pickax through his belt, and held his flashlight in his fist. He looked like a rebel ready for battle.

"Let's go," he said.

"Go where?" Becca asked.

"Inside. Right now," he responded with a nod.

"Son, come here," Clay said, holding out his hand.

Impatiently, Jimmy dashed up to him, and danced from one foot to the other.

"Jimmy, exactly what is it you think we're going to do?"

"Mom and Barry said we'd explore inside next time we came up here."

Clay's lips compressed and he gave Becca a quick, censoring frown. "I'm sorry, son, but you can't go in there without me." He tapped his cast. "And it will be a few weeks before I'll be in any shape to take you inside."

"Mom can do it."

"She's not dressed for it," Clay answered, indicating the long, loose sweater, slacks, and loafers.

Jimmy's lip stuck out and he gave his parents a look that accused them of betrayal.

"How come I have to wait for you to take me?"

"Because I'm a mining engineer, remember? I know about places like this, and I know they're dangerous."

That didn't mollify Jimmy at all. "Mom said," he insisted.

"Jimmy, when we left the house today, I didn't know you'd want to come up here," Becca pointed out reasonably. "Remember, I thought we were just coming for a drive and a, uh, snacknic."

Although he was irritated with his parents, they eventually soothed him with promises that as soon as Clay's leg was healed, they would explore the cave together, but not too far in.

"But I wanna know what's way down inside," he said.

"We'll find out together when you're older," Clay said calmly, but firmly. "And you're not to even *think* about going in by yourself."

It wasn't what he wanted, but Jimmy knew it was the best he was going to get, so he nodded, took another handful of cookies and ate them while he walked around the outside of the mine, picking up interesting rocks that he hoped were full of valuable ore and placing them in his backpack. Every once in a while, he would glance back at Clay and Becca and give a sigh as if asking why God had saddled him with such stick-in-the-mud parents.

By the time the shadows grew long, Jimmy was tired and Clay was drooping with fatigue. Becca hustled them back into the Explorer and drove home thinking that her plan to regain control of her little household was working quite well. She couldn't keep from thinking about the snatches of another Clay she'd seen, though, one who'd been a frightened little boy, and one who had wanted more children as badly as she had. In some ways, she felt as if the things she thought she knew about him, the things she'd taken for granted, had been shaken up.

"Are you sure you don't mind, Carol?" Becca stood on her friend's front porch and gave her a distressed look. Carol's son, Todd, was Jimmy's best friend and the two boys had planned a sleepover Becca had known nothing about.

She smiled ruefully at her friend, then looked down at Jimmy, who was loaded down with his usual amount of gear. Todd stood beside him, and both boys returned her look with a grin.

"Are you kidding?" Carol said. "These boys have been planning this sleepover for a week and it's never a problem to have Jimmy. They disappear into Todd's room and I don't see them again until they get hungry. It works out great."

"I just wish he'd told me about it."

Carol gave her a puzzled frown. "I called a couple of days ago to say I couldn't make it to your shower because my kindhearted boss loaded me down with a pile of paperwork and I have a major term paper due in my economics class, but I'd like to have Jimmy over. You didn't get the message?"

"N...o...o, can't say that I did," Becca answered. "I suppose it was Clay you spoke to?"

"That's right. It must have slipped his mind," Carol said. "Anyway, believe it or not, it's easier having two boys than one because Todd lets me get my work done if he's got someone to play with. Jimmy's dad said the sleepover tonight would be fine."

"I'll just bet he did," Becca muttered, then looked up with an apologetic smile. Carol was an easygoing single mother who worked in a local insurance office and took college classes whenever finances and time allowed. She didn't let little things upset her—a trait Becca knew she needed to cultivate. "Well, since it's all planned and you don't mind, I'm sure it will be okay."

The boys whooped, Jimmy gave her a quick hug, and they dashed toward Todd's room. With a laugh and a wave, Carol followed them. Becca turned away, going down the shallow steps of Carol's small house which was only a block away from hers. As she walked home, she thought back over the past week and tried to pinpoint a time when Clay had been home alone to take Carol's call. There had been several times, she recalled, because she'd run a few errands one day and she'd gone out with Barry twice.

She hadn't known a thing about it until she'd finished dressing for the bridal shower in her best black slacks and a green silk top. Jimmy had come from his room with his sleeping bag and a satchelful of toys to announce that he was ready for his sleepover. She hadn't been able to convince him to stay home, so they'd ended up at Carol's.

Becca was glad to let Jimmy stay, especially if it helped Carol out, but she felt disgruntled that Clay hadn't told her about it. She frowned at the cracks in the sidewalk and pulled her coat tightly around her as she stepped up her pace, knowing she had to get home soon because the guests would be arriving for the shower Lauren and Brittnie were throwing for her. As she walked, she mulled over the things that had been going on in her life.

In the week since their trip to the Lucy Belle, Clay had been more of an enigma than ever. He seemed to genuinely like Barry and the two men got along well. She didn't know why that should make her nervous, but it did.

Clay was making a good recovery. He had an appointment with Dr. Kress in a few days and if all was well, Becca intended to let him fend for himself while she returned to work. Surely he could complete his recovery without her constant attention.

Not that she had given him much attention lately. There had been no more afternoons of playing chess. She didn't want it to end the same way the last session had ended, with them kissing like a couple of hormone-saturated teenagers. She kept busy with all the little jobs she'd intended to do since moving into her house; preparing the soil for her garden, sewing new kitchen curtains, sorting old family pictures to go into albums which would then be presented to her stepmother and sisters for Christmas gifts.

Even that activity hadn't been much of an escape, though. She had frequently run across photos of her and Clay. There was one, taken soon after Jimmy's birth that had really touched her. In it, Clay had his arms around her and their newborn son. The love and pride his face had shown then had made her want to weep now. Where had it all gone wrong?

She knew they both shared the blame and she was afraid that the problems between them resembled a tapestry that was too complicated to unravel and too damaged to be worth saving.

Worst of all, she was spending all this time and energy thinking about a relationship she had thought was over. Strange behavior for a woman on the verge of marrying another man.

She hadn't wanted to think about that, so she'd kept herself busy and absorbed, and had avoided Clay as if he had been struck with a deadly virus rather than a broken leg. He seemed to know what she was doing, too. He watched her industriousness with an air of amusement, but he didn't say anything except to ask occasionally if she wasn't feeling a little tired.

Tired or not, she still had plenty of time to think, about Clay and his childhood, about the two babies she had miscarried and how it had affected both of them. She knew more now than she had when they'd been married, but she wasn't sure what to do with the information.

With a start, she realized she had reached her own front door and couldn't even remember the walk from Carol's house. Shaking her head, she hurried inside. She was going to talk to Clay about the undelivered phone message from Carol before the guests arrived.

Lauren had already been over to bring the refreshments and the decorations so the place looked very festive. The colors she and Barry had chosen for the simple wedding they were planning were mint green and peach. Streamers were swagged above the table which was covered in a cloth featuring that color scheme. Brittnie had ordered the cake from Dan's Bakery so they could taste it and decide if they wanted to order the wedding cake from him. They planned to save a large piece of this one for Barry. If the appearance matched the taste, it would be fabulous.

Becca looked around smiling, until she caught sight of the man sitting once again in the easy chair, his casted leg on the hassock, a delicate glass cup of punch held in his big miner's hand. He had cleaned up and shaved. Now he was dressed in a sports shirt and jeans with one leg cut off. He looked devilishly handsome.

"Clay, what do you think you're doing?"

"Drinking punch," he said, taking a sip. "Not bad, either, though it might benefit from a healthy slug of Scotch." He looked up. "Got any?"

She shuddered. "Certainly not."

"Don't sound like such a prude," he said in an injured tone. "I was just asking."

"Clay, you need to stay in your room tonight," she said through her teeth. "You're not invited to this."

"It's been a long time since I saw any of your relatives."

"I didn't know you were that wild to see them or I would have sent you to stay with one of them."

"Great idea." He grinned. "I choose your great-aunt Katrina. I hear she's coming."

Becca hadn't known that. No doubt it was another telephone message he'd neglected to deliver.

She decided to try a different approach. She took a breath and said in a reasonable tone, "Clay, it's a bridal shower, for goodness' sake!"

"What does it matter if I see all of your new finery?"

She rolled her eyes toward the ceiling. "I can't believe I'm explaining this, but ex-husbands aren't invited to bridal showers."

"A policy that stinks," he said, setting his cup on an end table. "I should think that it would help to have a man's opinion, even if it is your ex-husband's." He looked suddenly horrified. "Good lord, what if you end up with something in flannel? With little pink roses? It could be fatal to your marriage," he added in a worried tone.

"For your information, some men *like* their wives to wear flannel!"

Clay shook his head. "Don't believe it, honey. That's a lie put out by the flannel manufacturers' association. Those people will say anything to sell their product even if it wrecks marriages."

Becca stared at him. Clay was making a joke, and an incredibly silly one at that.

She shook her head and sputtered, "That is the craziest thing I've ever heard."

The doorbell rang and she gave it a frantically distracted look.

"Crazy or not, I'm staying right here." He clapped his hands on the arms of the chair. "I can't let you go through this alone. Better answer the door, Bec. Sounds like your guests are arriving.''

"Clay, I just don't know how we managed to miss meeting each other all these years.''

Becca glanced over her shoulder to see Hope Bishop, Barry's secretary, thorn in Becca's side at work, and unofficial Tarrant town flirt perched on the arm of Clay's chair. She was smiling down at him as if he was the most delicious thing she'd seen in a long time—which, of course, he probably was, considering the type of men Hope usually dated, Becca thought sourly.

Hope twirled one of her long red curls around her finger and gave Clay a coy look. "Why, I've known Becca for years, in fact, since before I started school. She was in junior high and she used to be my baby-sitter.''

Before Hope started school? Becca scoffed silently. That would be true only if Hope had waited until the age of ten to enter kindergarten. Becca, her baby-sitter? They had played together when Hope's father had brought her out to the ranch while he viewed cattle Hal was selling, but there hadn't been any baby-sitting involved.

It seemed that most of the women in the room, with the possible exception of her stepmother and sisters, had taken a look at Clay and allowed their good sense to have the weekend off. Even her great-aunt Katrina had greeted Clay as if he was her long-lost best friend.

Becca would have thought that all these women would be uncomfortable with a man joining them for a lingerie bridal shower, of all things, but everyone seemed to like having him there.

Especially Hope.

Becca glanced at her and Clay again just as Hope lifted her hands to fluff her long hair, which had been blond just a few weeks ago, and Clay looked up, catching Becca's eye. He gave her a wink, then turned his attention back to whatever inane thing Hope was saying.

Becca spun around and grabbed a cup of punch from the table, downing it quickly. The hot feeling rushing through her was *not* jealousy.

"This is weird beyond words," Shannon said as she walked up beside Becca and began selecting an assortment of finger sandwiches. Her long, dark hair hung in a satiny rope to her waist. She wore a dress of deep red knit that made her fair skin glow with a rosy richness. The dress was a nice change from the jeans and long-sleeved shirts she usually wore.

Becca knew that she and Brittnie were attractive women, but Shannon was stunning, even tonight with a slightly worried look on her face.

"You mean having Clay here? Don't I know it," Becca said morosely. She looked across the room at her stepmother who seemed to read her mind and answered her dismayed look with a sympathetic smile.

"It'll probably be in the *Tarrant Guardian*," Shannon went on, biting into a little cheese triangle. 'Ex-husband attends shower for former wife and fiancé—is the center of attention.'"

"Please, Shannon," Becca begged with a shudder. "Don't even suggest that. This is embarrassing enough as it is."

"Well, these women have known you all your life and they're real troupers. They won't act embarrassed if you don't. Although," she added, eyeing Clay and Hope. "There doesn't seem to be too much embarrassment around."

"They do seem to actually be enjoying him," Becca agreed sardonically.

"Well, bridal showers are usually pretty silly," Shannon said.

Becca smiled. She had always thought it was too bad that someone so beautiful didn't have a sentimental bone in her body.

"Maybe that's why everyone likes having him here. It's a novelty."

Shannon nodded. "What we need is a distraction. I'll get Lauren and tell her and Brittnie that we need to get on with the opening of the gifts."

Becca sighed as her sister moved away. She almost wished there was some way she could keep the gifts to open later, in private, without Clay's watchful eyes on her.

Just then, Clay tilted his head back and laughed at something Hope had said.

Maybe Becca wouldn't have to worry about Clay's eyes being on her. They seemed to be pretty well occupied with Hope.

Becca's great-aunt Katrina marched up to her. "Becca, sweetheart, I'm so glad to see you." She gave her niece a bone-cracking hug, which Becca returned. Katrina would never look her age. Any gray hair that dared to appear on her head was ruthlessly dyed a rich honey-blond. She acted and dressed young. In fact, tonight, she wore ankle boots with deep fringes, leggings, and a thick sweater of emerald green. "In fact," she went on. "I'm glad to see Clay, too, but this is the damnedest folderol I've ever heard of. What would the etiquette experts say about having your ex-husband at your bridal shower?"

"That's an interesting question coming from you.

You've never cared about anyone else's opinion, but if the experts met Clay, they probably would have kept their thoughts to themselves.''

Katrina gave a crack of laughter. "He is a little on the forceful side, isn't he?" She paused as she filled a plate with goodies. "Though, he seems to have changed. I've never seen him this friendly and relaxed before. Everyone's commented on it. What do you think it is, honey?"

Becca turned and tried to assess him dispassionately. He *was* relaxed, his expression openly warm and inviting. She had rarely seen him like this in their private moments, and never around other people. It wasn't that he'd actually disliked people. He was simply a loner who'd depended on himself for so long he hadn't felt the need to rely on others, or even to relate to them very much.

"I don't know, Aunt Katrina," she answered slowly. "Something about the accident seems to have changed him."

"For the better, I think. Do you regret divorcing him?"

"No," Becca said so quickly that her aunt raised an eyebrow at her. "Well, most of the time I don't."

"What I'm wondering is if you'll regret it after you marry Barry," Katrina said. "I've heard he's a nice boy but will he keep you warm where it counts?"

Becca's face flushed. "Aunt Kat, really, I...."

"Just something to think about," she said as she turned and bustled away.

This was turning out to be a heck of a bridal shower, Becca thought with deep irritation directed at Clay. The comparison Aunt Katrina was making was completely unfair because the two men were so different. And the differences wouldn't be so obvious if Clay had stayed in his room where he belonged.

Within a few minutes, Lauren, Shannon, and Brittnie had corralled the guests to sit down and watch as Becca opened her gifts. To Becca's amazement and relief, Clay stood, tucked his crutches under his arms, and prepared to leave the room. Hope Bishop's face fell, but Becca knew hers was full of relief because Clay gave her a wink as he maneuvered his way past the guests and left the room.

Murmuring that she needed to see if he was all right, Becca followed and caught up with him in front of his bedroom door. "Are you okay?" she asked.

"Never been better," he said as he thumped his way into his room. "But I knew you wouldn't want me there while you were opening up your new finery."

She blinked at him. "I...well, you're right. I'm just surprised you listened to me."

He turned and grinned at her. "Now, Bec, I'm not completely without manners. I just like to push your buttons sometimes."

"You mean you like to see me lose my temper," she said dryly. "I'm glad, though, that you're going to stay in here and not offer your opinions."

"Oh, I'll still offer my opinions. I'm expecting you to give me a fashion show when everyone's gone."

Her hands fell to her sides. "Are you crazy? I'll do no such thing."

"You could be making a mistake. What if a flannel granny gown slips through? Barry might not like it."

"I'm sure he can adjust," Becca snapped, turning and marching back to her guests.

Nerve, she thought, irritated with him all over again. Clay Saunders had way too much nerve.

* * *

The last guest finally left around ten o'clock. Becca's mother and sisters helped straighten up the house and clean the kitchen. When they departed, Becca was left with boxes of beautiful lingerie and the odd feeling that she was accepting these gifts under false pretenses. As she had opened each lovely gift, her friends had made jokes about how much Barry would like the item, but it was Clay's face she'd pictured.

To ease her conscience, she called Barry only to find that there was no answer. He'd probably turned off the bell on the phone and gone to bed. He went to bed early because he woke up early to go jogging. She didn't bother to leave a message, but hung up the receiver, picked up her gifts, and started for her room.

She tiptoed as she passed Clay's room, but he must have been lying awake in the dark, listening for her because he called out as she passed, "Anything you'd like to show me, Becca?"

With a sigh, she ignored him and kept right on walking. She deposited the packages on her bed. When she recrossed her room to close her bedroom door, she heard him coming down the hall. He hadn't been lying awake in the darkness. He'd probably been standing by the door, waiting for her to pass by.

She turned as he hopped into view in her doorway. He'd left his crutches behind, supporting himself against the wall as he moved. Now he stood with his arms stretched out on each side of him, his hands resting lightly on the doorjamb, balancing himself easily on his right leg.

His dark auburn hair was mussed and his eyes sleepy as if he'd just been awakened, though Becca knew that wasn't the case. His face was full of humor, which she suspected was at her expense, and his smile was cocky.

She was glad to see that he was still dressed in a sweat-shirt and a pair of cutoff jeans. If he'd shown up in the boxer shorts he usually slept in, she might have been…disturbed.

It showed how tired and distraught she was, that she was even considering the fact that he might be able to disturb her.

Readying for battle, she gave him a dismissive look. "Did you need something, Clay?"

"Just a look at your new honeymoon finery."

"Keep dreaming, buster," she said, efficiently stacking the boxes for storage in her closet.

"But I have been, Becca," he said, leaving the door-way and hopping lightly on one foot to the end of her bed. In spite of her armload of gifts and her irritation with him, she stepped forward automatically to offer help. He flashed a quick grin at her as he passed so close, he stirred the air around her. She gave him a disgruntled look. He should have looked silly hopping like that, but instead, he managed it with a certain amount of flair.

"In fact," he went on. "I've spent nearly two hours dreaming about this."

His words sent a strange little quiver through her. She shoved it down ruthlessly. He was nothing to her now—at least very little except that he was her son's father. The look she turned on him was cool. "Oh, re-ally?"

He tilted his head to the side. "Have you been prac-ticing that dismissive look and tone? I've never heard it before."

"I'm perfecting it just for you." She was quite pleased with the coolness in her voice.

He grinned and reached out. She tried to twirl away,

but he flipped the lid off the top box on the stack she held in her arms. Tucking a finger beneath the tissue paper, he reached in and snagged the thin spaghetti strap of the black lace teddy Aunt Kat had found for her at a little shop in Phoenix.

"Nice," he said appreciatively, though he actually saw little more than a blur because Becca dropped the load of packages onto the bed and made a grab for the teddy. She whipped it back into its box and clapped the lid on.

"This really isn't any of your business, Clay." Her voice was firm, grumpy, in fact, but she could feel the trembling of her fingers. She hoped he'd think it was from anger.

He didn't bother to answer. She knew she'd no doubt used that phrase so many times lately, he'd stopped responding to it.

"You never wore things like that when we were married," he said, instead.

"We met and married so quickly, there was no time for a bridal shower," she answered briskly, haphazardly gathering her new things and shoving them onto a closet shelf. They spilled, lovely colors and exquisite fabrics tumbling over each other. Desperately, she closed the door on them and turned back to Clay. She crossed her hands at her waist and gave him a steady look.

"That's not what I meant," he said. "You didn't have to receive things like that at a bridal shower to wear them for me. You could have bought them for yourself. Hell, I made plenty of money. You could have bought just about anything you wanted."

Except she never could have bought her way—begged, or blasted her way into a true understanding of him. Becca pushed that uncomfortable thought aside. It wasn't what they were discussing, and she didn't want to think about it just now.

"It wasn't about money, Clay," she said slowly.

"What was it about, Becca?" He took a step back and sat on her bed, scooting back far enough to give his leg some support. He looked at her with genuine curiosity, his full attention focused on her. For a moment, she didn't know what to say. This was the first time in nearly two years that they'd had a normal, adult conversation. Before they'd argued coldly, or lately, she'd been the object of his teasing.

Finally, she took a deep breath and said, "I'm a different person, now Clay. I'm going to marry someone else. He's easier to know, to...."

"Becca, you're getting off track," Clay's deep, inflexible voice broke in. "We're not talking about Barry here. We're talking about you and me."

"There is no you and me."

"Yes, Becca, there is," he said relentlessly. "And in one way or another, there always will be."

Becca looked down at her hands, which were held tightly together in front of her. She might as well tell him. He wouldn't leave until she did. She loosened her fingers, spread them out. "I wanted to wear those kinds of things," she admitted. "I wanted to be more...free, but it's hard." She looked up suddenly, her aquamarine eyes anguished. She was finally telling him something she'd never been able to say before. "Because I never felt like I really knew you."

His eyebrows drew together. "What?"

Becca's lips compressed, pulling together so hard her teeth ached. She stared at him while distressed thoughts whirled through her mind. She was about to tell him something she hadn't been able to admit, or to even articulate before.

She felt tears pinching at the back of her nose, then moving up to her eyes. She didn't want them to fall, but she didn't bother to fight them back. "For the five years we were actually together," she admitted. "I felt as if I was married to someone I didn't know, someone who kept himself locked away from me. I tried, I truly did, but I felt that there was always some part of you that was hidden away."

Clay stared at her for a long moment. "Come here, Becca."

"No, I really don't think that would be a good...."

"Come here, Becca," he repeated in a voice that told her that broken leg or no, he would come get her in a few seconds. She walked over to the bed. He reached out and pulled her down beside him, turning her so that she faced him. "You knew me, Becca. You knew all the important things about me. At least, you thought you did when you married me."

"No, I didn't."

"Then you've developed a faulty memory." His lips quirked. "But I noticed that the other day when I kissed you."

Her defiant look told him she wasn't going to rise to that bait. Instead, she said, "I didn't know you because everything happened too quickly between us, and throughout our marriage, it was as if we never caught up. We didn't date. We didn't court. We fell right into lust. We married and became parents within a year."

"Lots of people do that," he pointed out dryly.

"Those people must know each other better than you and I did."

"Maybe, or maybe they're willing to stay together and work things out when they get rough."

At a loss, she shook her head. He might be listening, but he wasn't hearing her. How could they have known each other as well as they needed to when she'd never known what he was thinking?

When she couldn't answer, he went on, "It happened fast because it was right, Becca. You can deny it all you want, you can have bridal showers and pick out colors and choose bakeries for your wedding cake, and make wedding plans, but that will never change what was between us."

His voice had deepened so that it seemed to fill her head. Becca met his eyes, which weren't arrogant as she had expected, but which moved with an expression that reminded her of the day of the accident, when he'd awakened in the hospital and looked at her with such joy.

Reaching out, Clay took her chin in his hand. His thumb ran over her lips and Becca's mouth trembled open on a sigh. The familiar warmth of his touch melted through her, making her wish that things really were right between them—the way he said they had been.

"Clay, maybe you're…you're right," she said in a shaky voice. "But that doesn't change the past and…and we have no future…except where…" She stopped to swallow hard. "Except where Jimmy is concerned."

Clay's hand went still, then dropped away. His breath puffed out in a derisive burst. "If you think that, Becca, you're not nearly as smart as I always thought you were."

Gently, he pushed her away from him and stood up. "You're fighting awfully hard, Bec, but I don't know who it is you're fighting."

He left the room, awkwardly this time, seeming to have lost the easy motion he'd had before. The soft thump of his foot sounded on the hardwood floor and she heard his hands sliding along the walls, keeping him upright. In a moment, Becca heard his door shut with a click.

She put her hands over her face and held them there, trying to bring her riotous emotions back under control. There was a grain of truth in what he said; there had been something very right between them at first, but it had gone awry. It must have, because otherwise, she would still be married to him, they would have a home together with their son, and she wouldn't be sitting alone on her bed wondering where her life had taken a wrong turn.

CHAPTER SEVEN

"WELCOME back, Becca," Hope Bishop called out as Becca entered the offices of the Tarrant Chamber of Commerce the next Monday. Before Becca could take off her coat and put away her purse, Hope hurried over and said, "How is Clay? Well enough to be left alone, hmm?"

Becca gave the other woman a dubious look. In spite of the fifty degree temperature outside, Hope was wearing a powder blue suit with a very short skirt, while Becca was sensibly dressed in boots, a pullover sweater, and a calf-length wool skirt. She certainly didn't think Hope's concern was for Clay's health. "He's well enough so that I don't have to be there all the time. He can take care of himself."

Hope smiled. "Yes, I guess he can. I'd think a hunk like him could do anything."

Including see right through a woman like Hope, Becca noted uncharitably. Instead of speaking that thought, she gave Hope a stiff little smile and turned to remove her coat and hang it on the wooden coat tree at the end of her desk.

"Say, Becca, we've known each other for a long time...."

Becca lifted an eyebrow at her. "You mean since the days when I baby-sat you?"

Hope had the grace to blush a little bit. "Well, you know a woman has to say whatever she needs to in order to get a man to notice her."

"Oh, yes," Becca answered dryly. "Stretching the truth is always a good tactic."

Oblivious to the irony in Becca's comment, the other woman nodded. "That's what I thought."

Becca rolled her eyes, but Hope didn't notice. She barreled ahead. "So let me ask you something. Why, exactly, did you divorce Clay?"

Stunned, Becca gaped at her. "What?"

"I mean, he didn't cheat on you or anything, did he?"

"Certainly not!"

The secretary looked pleased and relieved. "Well, that's good. I mean, I'd hate to think you'd been married to a guy who chased other women. So, the divorce must have been your fault then, huh?"

Becca opened her mouth, but it was a few seconds before she could force the words out. Finally, she said, "Hope, the reasons for my divorce are none of your business."

Hope waved her hands carelessly. "Oh, yeah, I know, I know. My mom says I'm always sticking my nose in where it doesn't belong. But I just want to make sure it's all over between you, that you two aren't still in love. I mean, I might be interested in going after Clay myself, you know?"

Becca felt as if she'd taken a leap into another dimension. She couldn't even form words to tell Hope how rudely she was behaving. "I can't believe this," she said.

"Why not?" Hope asked. "He's still a good-looking guy and I bet he makes good money, too. And living all over the country, even the world—that must be exciting."

Flabbergasted, Becca could only stare.

Hope gave her an exasperated look. "Becca, everything's over between you, isn't it?" the girl urged. "I mean, even though he's been living with you, it's not like you're still interested—after all, you're going to marry the boss."

"Whether I'm still interested or not doesn't matter," Becca answered, her voice reedy with shock.

"Nah, I know it doesn't," Hope said, giving her a big, airy smile. "I just thought it would be more polite to ask." She swung away, heading back to her own desk outside Barry's small office. "I'd better get back to work 'cause the boss gets really mad if I goof off."

As Hope spun away, Becca reached out as if to grab her by the arm and give her a shake, but she clutched only air. The empty-headed twit simply didn't understand. How could she, when she didn't listen?

With a sound of hopeless frustration, Becca dropped her hand and returned to her own desk, grateful for the five-foot-high divider that separated her from the rest of the office. Maybe she couldn't really blame Hope. The kind of situation Becca found herself in did seem to invite questions, although most people were too polite to ask them.

Becca sat down and looked at the pile of mail on her desk. She was glad to see it. The work it involved would keep her busy all day, helping her justify to herself that she'd returned to work before she'd planned.

It was true that Clay was doing well, she thought as she picked up her letter opener and began applying it to the stack of envelopes. He didn't really need her help anymore at all, not even to get around the house. He'd proven that when he'd hopped into her room the night of the shower. The real reason she'd returned to work was because she just didn't want to be alone with him anymore. It had been different when his broken leg had kept him bedfast, or wheelchair bound, but for the past couple of days he seemed to be everywhere she was, so she'd simply left. Run away.

Obviously, she didn't have to worry about Jimmy, either. If his dad was home when he got there, the boy was ecstatically happy.

In fact, she was the only person in their little threesome who wasn't happy. The situation was very similar to what it had been when she had left Clay, only now he seemed to be more open to listening to her—when he wasn't intent on telling her how she should be feeling, or should be reconsidering her choices.

He had said she was fighting awfully hard, but he didn't know who she was fighting.

She *wasn't* fighting. She was going straight ahead with the plans she was making for a safe and secure future with Barry for her and Jimmy.

She had seen Barry the night before and she'd told him she was ready to come back to work. Although he'd given her a long look, he hadn't questioned her choice. A major difference from Clay who questioned everything about her.

Becca switched on her computer in preparation for answering some of her mail, but she paused as she reached for the first letter on the stack. She had to admit that Clay's pushy questions had the effect on her of forcing her to clarify her thinking. She now understood her reasons for divorcing him better than she had when the event had actually taken place. She had the sudden, uncomfortable thought that maybe that's what partners were supposed to do; to help each other focus their thinking.

Barry, on the other hand, accepted whatever she said or did with easygoing grace. It had a calming effect on her. Didn't that prove he loved her? That he was right for her?

Unexpectedly, the thought came that maybe it was too calming. Her dad had always told her that worthwhile things were much more trouble. Anything that came too easily didn't have much value. Becca admitted that she liked being with Barry precisely because he was so easy-going and understanding. But didn't she deserve that, after her years with Clay?

Before she could continue with her endless round of thinking, Barry came into the office. He walked straight over to talk to her and welcome her back to work.

She smiled at him. He was so solid and dependable. When she was with him, she never felt the tumult of emotions she invariably experienced with Clay.

"If you're free for lunch," he said. "Let's go over to Pearl's." He glanced at Hope who was busily filing some papers, and straining her ears to hear every word of their conversation. "I need to talk to you."

"Sure, Barry. I'd like that."

The three of them worked all morning without exchanging more than a few words. Becca was glad to be back, and to be involved in projects that kept her from thinking about Clay.

At lunchtime, she and Barry walked down the street to Pearl's Restaurant. Typical of a small-town eating establishment, it had a menu that catered heavily to beef lovers and to those who didn't give a thought to their cholesterol levels. Pearl also made the best pies in the county and sliced the pieces in generous portions.

They found a booth at the back and ordered the lunch special which Pearl delivered in record time. As they were finishing, Barry looked across the table at Becca and said, "I know we talked about setting our wedding date for the end of May, but I think we ought to move it up.''

Becca set the remainder of her hamburger down on her plate and said, "Move it up?" She couldn't have explained the unexpected sense of alarm that shot through her.

"Yes." He reached across the table and took her hand. "I was thinking of May first."

"That's only five weeks away." She winced at the thinness of her voice. Grabbing her glass, she swallowed some cola.

His brow wrinkled. "The panicked tone in your voice doesn't exactly fill me with confidence, Rebecca. Haven't changed your mind, have you?"

"No, no," she said hastily. She shook her head so vigorously her French braid swished against the back of her chair. "It's just that it's a little...sudden. I didn't know you were thinking of moving the date up."

"That's why I'm telling you now," he answered reasonably. "We still have plenty of time to make wedding plans, don't you think? I mean since we only want a small wedding."

"Well, yes, I suppose so." She hadn't anticipated this. She'd expected to have a little more time in which to make plans for the wedding day. An uncomfortable thought surfaced that she might really be more interested in anticipating the wedding than in actually planning it.

Barry, who usually went along happily with whatever she requested, gave her a shrewd look. "How long did you think we should be engaged before actually getting married?"

Years was the word that popped to the front of her mind, then she was appalled at herself for even thinking it. "Uh, well, I'm not sure," she hedged. "For a while,

I suppose." Lame, she thought as she watched the puzzlement on his face. Really lame. She gave him a sickly smile, which he didn't return.

"Rebecca, I don't want to be engaged for 'a while.' If you're not sure about this...."

"I am," she said hastily. She had a vision of Clay saying, "I told you so." She wasn't going to let that happen.

"Well, then?" Barry asked.

"May first sounds great." She hoped she sounded enthusiastic.

"Then it's settled," he said quickly. "We'll be married on May first in your home." He paused. "Uh, you don't think Clay will be interested in attending, do you?"

Becca opened her mouth to say nothing could induce him to attend, but then all she could do was sigh. She was afraid that Clay would delight in attending the ceremony, and possibly in trying to stop it.

For the first time, Becca experienced the feeling that she was being disloyal or unfaithful to Clay by making plans to marry Barry.

The dismay on her face must have been obvious because Barry said, "Well, we'll worry about that when we have to. In the meantime, my parents want to come down from Denver to meet you and Jimmy."

At the mention of her son's name, Becca felt herself going pale. Jimmy. She hadn't told him yet that she and Barry were getting married. She had hoped to break the news gently, once Clay was out of the house. If they moved the wedding date up, she would no longer have that option. She had to talk to him right away, but she also had to choose exactly the right moment. Thank goodness, Clay had decided to keep quiet about it and let her tell their son in her own time.

She chewed on her lip as she mulled it over. She and Clay had always given important news to Jimmy together. When her father had died, the three of them had sat, hugging each other, while Clay had calmly explained to their son that he wouldn't be seeing Grandpa anymore. That had made it easier for Jimmy to understand.

The news of her marriage to Barry wasn't something she could ask her ex-husband to share with their son, however. She would do it today.

"Becca, is something wrong?"

She looked up and blinked at Barry's worried face. "What?"

"My parents? Meeting you and Jimmy."

"Oh, oh, of course. I'd like to meet them, too. When?"

"This weekend."

Becca thought it over and made a quick decision. How could she ever explain the presence of her ex-husband? "I think it would be best if we didn't meet at my house."

Barry nodded. "I understand. I'll pick the two of you up. We can meet them for lunch, then go back to my apartment for coffee."

His small apartment wouldn't be nearly as comfortable for them all as her home, but Becca appreciated his thoughtfulness. She nodded. "I think that sounds fine, Barry. I'm looking forward to meeting them."

He smiled at her and finished his lunch, but Becca pushed hers away. She was full, and besides, she had too much to think about to concentrate on food. She was very fond of Barry and wondered why she was questioning her commitment to him. She decided that after work, she would go out to the family ranch and discuss all of this with her stepmother. Then she would get her son alone that evening and explain all about her remarriage.

The Kelleher family had owned the ranch at the junction of the Gregg and Star Rivers for nearly eighty years. Her great-grandparents had been among Tarrant Valley's pioneers and family legend had it that her great-grandmother Catherine had endured such a miserable trip by wagon all the way from Kansas that she'd sworn she would settle in the first place she saw once they reached Colorado. They'd crossed the border in the night, winding slowly over a narrow dirt road, following the sound of the running water. When dawn broke, Catherine had seen the perfect spot for her home, at the base of a granite knoll, surrounded by cedar trees. She refused to go another inch and had begun unloading the wagon immediately while her husband, James, had pleaded with her to continue. The tract of land they'd bought was further up the valley.

Catherine had held her ground, literally, and James had finally traded for the place she wanted, though they'd both learned later that the cedars were a magnet for gnats and mayflies. No matter, the little house James had built her was her pride and the ranch had prospered.

It had come to Becca's grandfather, then to her father. None of Hal Kelleher's daughters wanted the place for themselves, but Jimmy loved it. Mary Jane encouraged his interest, so someday the place might come to him, continuing the tradition.

Becca drove up in front of the house just as Mary Jane emerged from the barn. She was removing her work gloves and examining her hand. Seeing Becca, she smiled and waved. When she did so, Becca noticed that there was an angry red mark across her palm.

"What have you done now?" she asked. Mary Jane was a little bit accident prone. She had numerous scars from her encounters with cattle and ranch equipment over the years.

Mary Jane shrugged. "Picked up a piece of iron that was sharper than it looked," she answered. "It cut clean through this old glove of mine, but it barely scratched my palm. Thought I could use the iron to reinforce a fence post over on the west pasture."

"*I* thought you were going to let the fence repairs wait a week or two."

"I was," Mary Jane said, looking up with a quirky smile. "But this one can't wait. Mr. Blackhawk called to tell me about it."

Becca snorted derisively. "And no doubt threatened you with the sheriff if it wasn't fixed to his liking."

Mary Jane's rueful look answered for her.

"I don't know why he says things like that," Becca continued hotly. "He knows Kent Drucker wouldn't bother with a nuisance complaint like that. Besides, Kent's your cousin."

"Which is why Kent would have to investigate, to avoid accusations of family favoritism." Mary Jane climbed the back steps and swung open the door. "Believe me, honey, it's easier to just fix the darned fence post."

"Mr. Blackhawk's an old crab," Becca said, stepping into the kitchen. It was as sparkling clean and neat as always. Though she'd only been six when her father had married Mary Jane, she remembered what the place had looked like before, with dirty dishes piled everywhere and a floor so grimy damp boots left mud trails. Mary Jane had whipped through the place like a tornado, leaving clean orderliness in her path. Becca marveled at it now because Mary Jane had been all of eighteen at the time.

"A rich old crab," Mary Jane answered, bringing Becca back to the discussion. "Which I guess is why he thinks he can have everything his own way."

"I don't know about that," Becca said, picking up the teakettle and filling it with water for tea. "I met many wealthy people through Clay's work and I never saw anyone like old Augustus Blackhawk."

"There *is* no one like him." Mary Jane washed her hands, spread some antiseptic cream on the scrape, then got a small plastic bag of ice from the refrigerator to hold against her palm. She kept a supply of such bags ready for use.

"Thank goodness," Becca answered.

For as long as she could remember, their family had been in one minor conflict or another with their neighbor, Gus Blackhawk. Her parents hadn't said much about it except to speculate that he was a bitter, unhappy old man who'd succeeded in driving away his only son so he was mad at the world. As far as she knew, the son had never even been home to visit.

"Was his son like that?"

Mary Jane adjusted the ice bag before she answered. "His son? You mean Garrett?"

"That's right. You were in school with him, weren't you?"

"Yes. He left right after high school graduation. Joined the Army." Mary Jane looked down again and shook her head. "No, Garrett wasn't like that at all."

"He probably joined up to avoid his father."

"Something like that," Mary Jane admitted. Her voice was strained and Becca gave her a curious look.

"Does your hand hurt?"

"No, no. I'm fine. Forget about Old Gus," Mary Jane commanded, her voice full of hearty cheerfulness. "Tell me how my grandson is, and how's Clay?"

"They're both doing all right," Becca answered, turning away to find the teapot and the box of tea bags.

"Then tell me how *you* are."

Becca's laughter was soft, and directed at herself. "Well, Mom, I don't really know." As she made tea, she told Mary Jane about the doubts she was having, and about the changes in Clay that made her wonder if she was doing the right thing. When she was finished with her monologue, she brought the teapot and two cups to the table, poured for both of them, sat down opposite her stepmother and said, "What should I do?"

Mary Jane laughed. "You're asking the wrong person. You should be asking that of yourself. I can't tell you what to do, only that you can't drag your feelings for one man into your marriage to another." She looked down suddenly, frowning at the tabletop. Her hands, which were cradling the cup of tea tightened for a moment. "It just doesn't work if you try that, honey. You've got to resolve one relationship before you commit yourself to the next one."

The tone in her voice caught Becca off guard. It sounded very…personal, but Becca knew Mary Jane's commitment to Hal had been total. She'd married him within weeks of graduating from high school, so there probably hadn't been time for a serious relationship before that. On the other hand, how did she know? Mary Jane's childhood had been extremely unhappy and she'd no doubt been delighted to escape it by marrying Hal.

She had rarely talked about her younger life to Becca. There might have been someone Mary Jane had loved, but Becca didn't know.

Mary Jane looked up suddenly and Becca thought of how young and pretty she was and how much Becca admired her for the way she was pushing herself to keep the ranch going.

"I wish I was wise enough to tell you what to do, how to resolve this," her stepmother said. "But you have to do it yourself."

"I guess I knew that," Becca answered wryly. "Maybe all these strange feelings are being caused because he seems so different, and because he's close now."

"Maybe. And maybe there's more going on in your head, and in your heart, than you want to acknowledge."

"No," Becca answered stubbornly. "I'm sure that when he goes to Venezuela, I'll get back to normal."

Mary Jane picked up her cup and looked at her step-daughter over its rim. "Maybe. But what exactly is normal?"

"What do you mean?"

Mary Jane toyed with her cup for a few seconds before answering. "Since I'm only twelve years older than you, I feel in some ways that we grew up together. You're my daughter, but you're also like a sister to me, so I know you in many different ways, and I know you're very stubborn."

Becca couldn't deny that. She kept quiet and waited for her to go on.

"Frankly, honey, I'm wondering whether you're more committed to marrying Barry or to showing Clay that you're getting on with your life—without him."

Dismayed, Becca shook her head. "Oh, no, that's not why I'm marrying Barry," she said quickly.

Mary Jane spread her hands on the table. "Then I guess I don't know why you're doing it. Your dad and I were surprised when you married Clay so suddenly, but we knew it was because you were crazy about him. I'm wondering where that kind of craziness is in your relationship with Barry."

Becca opened her mouth, but nothing came out except, "I don't know. I suppose since things didn't work out with Clay, I didn't think I should get crazy like that again."

"Becca, you always need a little of that in your marriage or you get darned bored."

Distressed, Becca could only shake her head. Mary Jane took pity on her and changed the subject. They talked about other things until Becca was ready to leave.

With her arm around Becca's waist, Mary Jane walked her to the car. "What you've got to decide is what you really want."

Becca gave her a dismayed look. "I thought the divorce was what I wanted, but now...Clay's different...."

"And so are you. You're the one who has to decide if that's a good thing or a bad one, but frankly, Becca, I think you've left this soul-searching a bit late. Here you are on the verge of marrying another man."

Becca winced. "I know."

Mary smiled sympathetically, gave Becca a hug, then watched as she drove away.

Becca decided that she would deal with this calmly and rationally. She was sure she was doing the right thing. She and Barry got along very well. They never argued and she and Clay had—or at least she had tried to argue and Clay had answered her with cold logic.

There was peace between her and Barry. Mary Jane was wrong. She didn't need craziness in a marriage. She needed peace, calmness, and predictability.

She would talk to Jimmy about her remarriage. He liked Barry. Surely it wouldn't be too hard for him to accept. Another thing she would do was to stop letting her lingering feelings for Clay cloud her thinking.

The breakup of her marriage to him was in the past. She would no longer worry and obsess over it. What she had told her mom was true. She only spent so much time thinking about him and doubting herself because he was living in her house. Once he was gone, she would no longer have these doubts and troubled feelings. In fact, he would live his life, she would live hers, and the only thing they would share was Jimmy.

She was quite pleased with this rational conclusion. Her resolution lasted until she walked in her own front door and found Hope Bishop trying to wiggle her way onto Clay's lap.

CHAPTER EIGHT

HOPE was still wearing the suit she'd worn to work that day but she'd discarded the jacket. It was tossed on Becca's sofa and her clingy white blouse was unbuttoned a few more buttons than it had been at work. Hope, herself, was perched on the arm of Clay's chair, one hand resting along the back, the other on his shoulder as if she was trying to hold him in place.

Not that it was necessary, Becca concluded, as her stunned surprise gave way to a jolt of heat that had her slamming the door and striding into the room. Clay didn't look like he was anxious to get away from Hope's clutches.

"Am I interrupting something?" Becca asked. She didn't know where her strident tone of voice had come from, but she didn't try to cool it down.

Hope sprang up from the arm of Clay's chair. One hand flew up to smooth her hair and the other swept down to tug at her skirt. She couldn't get the alarm off of her face fast enough, though, and her voice shot up to a tinkling soprano. "Oh, hi, Becca. I thought you'd gone out with the boss for dinner." She gestured to the man in the chair whose face was beginning to break into a grin. "Clay thought so, too."

Becca gave Clay a narrow-eyed look. Clay had known she wasn't going out with Barry tonight.

"No, Barry and I didn't have plans for the evening," she said tightly, indicating the bag of groceries in her arms.

"Oh, uh-huh. I see. Well, after we talked this morning, I didn't think you'd mind if I came over."

Becca scowled at her. Something in her expression must be getting through to Hope if the nervous twitch of her eyes was any indication. Becca decided she should have tried this approach earlier in the day. "You thought wrong," she said sweetly, but her aquamarine eyes were sharp.

Hope gulped and Clay reached up to cover his mouth with his hand.

Becca gave him a dour look. She had a pound of ground beef in her grocery bag. If Clay was laughing at her, he was going to get the meat right in the place that was smirking at her.

"Oh, well, I guess I misunderstood."

"I guess you did."

"I'll be going then," Hope stammered. She looked down at Clay. "I'll see you later."

"Sure, Hope," he answered as she snatched up her suit jacket and purse and scurried for the door.

When it shut behind the fleeing girl, Becca rolled her eyes at him. "Really, Clay." She started for the kitchen.

"Wait a minute, Miss High and Mighty," Clay said. His fist swooped down and snagged one of his crutches. With one hand he held the top and with the other he held the crossbrace and thumped the end down on the top of the coffee table. Becca slammed up against it and nearly went sprawling.

"Clay!"

"What was that all about?"

She righted herself and fumbled her bag of groceries upright. "I don't know what you mean."

"Oh, come off it," he scoffed. "I want to know what you and the luscious Miss Bishop were talking about."

"Only a conversation we had in the office this morning. It doesn't concern you."

"Like hell, it doesn't."

Becca stared at him. He was as intent on knowing as she was on keeping him from knowing. Calmly, she gathered her skirt to her knee, stepped over the crutch, and proceeded to the kitchen. In a few seconds, she heard him stomping along right behind her. She thumped her grocery bag down on the counter and began plucking out meat, bread, and vegetables.

"Becca, you might as well tell me," Clay said, appearing in the doorway.

She toyed with the idea of refusing, but she, of all people, knew how tenacious he could be. With a look that told him she was doing this just to shut him up, she said, "Oh, all right. It appears that Hope is romantically interested in you. This morning at work, she asked if the divorce had been your fault."

"To which you immediately said, 'Certainly not!' Right, Bec?"

Becca ignored him. "She's decided she wants to 'go after' you."

Clay's grin broke out again. "No kidding?"

"Would I kid about something like that? She thinks you're a hunk." Becca slapped a few more groceries on the counter. "And from what I saw, she didn't waste any time showing you just how much of a hunk you are."

Clay leaned against the counter and crossed his arms over his crutches. "Becca, that wasn't what it seemed to be."

She turned away to place some items in the refrigerator, but glanced back over her shoulder. "That claim doesn't hold much water since you've still got her lipstick all over your mouth."

He reached for a paper towel, swiped his mouth, then examined the smear of coral. "Hey, she kissed me. I didn't kiss her."

"Oh, that's a very fine distinction. You weren't exactly fighting her off." Becca slammed the refrigerator door.

"Why would I need to? You came home just in time to do it for me."

"I guess it's a lucky thing I did, too, because...." She paused with a can of tomato sauce in her hand as she realized exactly where she was going with that statement. She sounded exactly like a jealous wife!

"Because why, Becca?" Clay asked, reaching out to remove the can and set it gingerly on the counter. His dark green eyes were full of devilish laughter. His mouth quivered with it.

Her lips clamped together and she lifted her chin. "Never mind, Clay."

"Becca, I know it's possible that I've been confined so long that I've got a bad case of cabin fever, but I think I just heard something in your voice I've never heard before."

"And what would that be?" she asked, feigning boredom. Darn it! Why couldn't she have acted like she didn't care? Why had she been foolish enough to make a scene?

Grinning, he reached up and tugged on his ear. "I think it was jealousy."

"Don't be ridiculous, Clay."

"No, no seriously. I'm just about positive that's what I heard."

Knowing she was failing in trying to ignore him and

downplay her reaction, Becca turned to face it head-on. "Clay, if you and your new girlfriend want to play footsie, that's your business, but this is my house and I don't want such things going on here, especially not in front of my son."

Clay burst out laughing. The sound rattled the pre-Depression glass on the display shelves. "Footsie? Honey, she was intent on a lot more than footsie."

Becca's face burned. "You know what I mean."

"Becca, for one thing, our son is over at Todd's house watching cartoons. For another, doesn't it occur to you that this sounds an awful lot like a conversation you and I had about three weeks ago?"

"What do you mean?"

He leaned over and tapped the cast on his leg. "I mean the day of the accident when I learned about you and Barry."

Becca stared at him. Now she didn't know what to say. She didn't want to admit that she had been jealous. What's more, she *really* didn't want to know that he'd been jealous when he'd learned of her plans to marry Barry. She wanted only to end this conversation. She cleared her throat. "Oh, yes, I see where there might be some similarities in the situation."

"Similarities." Clay shook his head. "I'm constantly amazed at your powers of self-delusion. There's a lot more going on here than a few similarities."

Becca pressed her fingers against the edge of the counter. She didn't look at him, wouldn't answer.

He adjusted the crutches and turned away. "There's a basketball game I want to watch."

He left the kitchen but Becca stayed rooted where she was. He was right. She was jealous. In fact, the hot searing jealousy that had shot through her when she'd walked in and found Hope there had rocked her right down to the soles of her boots.

Becca picked up the paper towel Clay had used to wipe the lipstick from his mouth and began shredding it with jerky little motions.

She had no right to be jealous if he was with another woman, or envious, or any other emotion. She had been the one to file for divorce, to meet another man and decide to marry him, to move ahead with her life. A sick feeling settled in the pit of her stomach. For the first time, she allowed the doubts to surface. Had she done the wrong thing? If she reacted this strongly, maybe there was more going on than she realized—at least more going on inside herself.

Dinner was very strained that evening. Becca was busy with her own thoughts, shaken by what she had realized. Clay didn't say very much. He watched her, though he wasn't laughing at her now. His expression was one of watchful expectation.

Jimmy chattered about his day, telling them in detail about the cartoons he and Todd had watched, which seemed to consist mostly of fight scenes between slimy alien creatures.

Becca finally came out of her self-absorption long enough to focus on what Jimmy was saying. She gave him a worried frown. "Jimmy, those cartoons sound pretty violent, not like what Carol would usually let you two watch."

Realizing he'd told on himself, Jimmy looked down at his plate. "She was, uh, busy working at her computer." To redeem himself, he quickly ate two green beans.

Becca's stern look told him this couldn't be solved by dutifully downing his vegetables. "You know which cartoons you're allowed to watch and which ones you're not."

Jimmy's bottom lip stuck out. "Yes, Mom," he answered, but he didn't say it with much conviction.

"Next time, I think you and Todd had better watch cartoons over here. Todd's mom could probably use a break from watching the two of you."

"Okay," Jimmy answered, relieved that he'd escaped a reprimand so easily. He finished eating his dinner and scampered off to his room.

Clay gave her a questioning look as if he was wondering what was going on in her mind. Ordinarily, she would have been a little more firm in her punishment. She knew that was true, but right now she had too many other things to think about.

She cleared the table, lingered over washing the dishes, and then took a deep breath as she slipped into Jimmy's room. He was sitting on the floor surrounded by his military action figures who appeared to be refighting the Gulf War.

"Finished with your homework?" she asked.

He sat up. "Yeah. Dad checked it."

"Okay." Becca sat down on the bed and patted the space beside her. "Come here, honey."

Dutifully, Jimmy stood and climbed onto the bed. He leaned up against her and she snuggled him close, glad that he was still young enough not to be embarrassed by gestures of affection from his mother.

"Sweetheart, you like Barry, don't you?"

"Sure, he's cool."

Pleased by this response, Becca continued. "You know Barry likes you, too. He and I have been seeing a lot of each other."

Jimmy gave her a puzzled look that told her he didn't

understand. "I mean he and I like each other very much. We like to be together, and we'd like to be together all the time."

"Oh," her son responded blankly. "You mean, he'll come over more and be friends with you and me and Dad?"

She was doing a bad job of this, she knew, but she struggled on. "Well, not exactly. You see, honey, Barry and I are going to get married."

As she watched apprehensively, Jimmy's face changed in a way she'd never seen before. His nose wrinkled up, his mouth opened, and he fell back on the bed giggling.

"Mom, you're silly. You can't do that. Dad won't let you." He broke into fresh bursts of hilarity.

Nonplussed, Becca stared at her son. She didn't know what to say. She certainly hadn't anticipated this reaction. "Jimmy, it's true," she said doggedly. "Barry and I are going to be married. He'll live here with us."

Jimmy stopped laughing, sat up, and said, "You mean he'll have Dad's room and Dad will be in your room again?"

"No, no, honey. Dad won't be here...."

"Where'll he be? He told me he's not going to Belezella."

"Venezuela," she corrected. "No, he's not going there, at least not for a while."

"Then he'll be here with us," Jimmy said with unshakable, simple faith.

She tried. For another ten minutes, Becca tried to explain, but Jimmy either couldn't or wouldn't understand and she finally gave up.

Leaving his room, she berated herself for the mess she'd made of things. If she'd told Jimmy as soon as she had accepted Barry's proposal, this wouldn't be happening now. She had thought she was easing him into the notion, accustoming him to the idea of having Barry for a stepfather, but she'd really been ducking the situation.

Or maybe she'd been lying to herself, she thought uncomfortably as she walked into her own room. It had been easy to tell herself, her family, her friends that she was going to marry Barry. Everyone had been willing to go along with her, to make plans, to be happy for her. She hadn't told Jimmy because there was no way she could look into those deep green eyes of his and tell anything less than the truth. She had never lied to her son. Neither had she ever been able to lie to Clay. That's probably why she'd put off telling him about her and Barry.

She didn't want to face that about herself, so she found some busywork to do folding laundry, then spent the evening reading a book. She and Clay hardly spoke, which was a relief, because she really didn't want to get into any more conversations that would make her question herself and her decisions. She felt him watching her, though, and looked up several times to meet his eyes and see the curiosity there.

As had become their custom, the two of them put Jimmy to bed. Their son seemed to have forgotten about the conversation she'd had with him. Either that, or he'd decided to ignore it, in effect, ducking some thing he didn't want to face. Becca winced inwardly. Like mother like son.

When she and Clay started down the hallway, to go into their separate rooms, Clay stopped Becca by putting a hand on her arm.

"Becca, we need to talk." His tone was serious, as was his expression.

She shook her head. "I don't think so, Clay. Today was my first day back at work. I'm very tired, so I'm going to bed."

The truth was, she simply couldn't handle any serious conversations, especially if they led to even more self-doubt and soul-searching.

Clay stood looking down at her, his hand warm and possessive on her arm. "I never would have believed I could be so patient," he said softly. "I didn't think it was in my nature."

His statement was so unexpected, her head snapped up. "What are you talking about? Patient over what?"

"With you, of course." He lifted his hand and ran one finger down her cheek.

Becca shivered and he smiled, a slow, sexy smile that sent her heart skipping. Oh, no, she thought. Oh, no. This wasn't supposed to happen. She wasn't supposed to start having these physical reactions to him again. She'd been so careful to keep them under control. Even when he'd kissed her, she hadn't let it affect her. At least, not too much.

Her lips trembled when she asked, "Why would you need to be patient with me?"

"Because I've been waiting for you to figure out exactly what it is that you want." His hand settled on her cheek once again.

"I know what I want." She batted his hand away. The touch was too familiar, too precious. The last thing she wanted.

His hand dropped away, but he didn't move. "You're making this awfully hard on yourself, Becca."

Tightness closed around Becca's heart, squeezing as

if trying to wring tears from her. "I don't know what you're talking about, Clay. Anymore it's...it's impossible to talk to you."

"You don't talk, Becca," he answered harshly. "You run, duck, and hide."

Denials sprang to her lips, but she bit them back. She wanted this to end and if she answered, it would continue. Two people were necessary for an argument, but if one walked away, the argument would end.

She didn't want an argument from him. She didn't want anything.

Her eyes lifted to his. Everything that had happened today ran through her mind. She recalled what her stepmother had told her about being finished with one relationship before beginning another and about her own stubbornness. The problem was, Becca wasn't sure she would ever be finished with her connection to Clay Saunders—and there was something about him that fueled her stubbornness.

"I told Jimmy that Barry and I are going to get married," she said rashly.

Clay went still. "Oh? How did he take it?"

"Very well."

"Turned handsprings, did he?"

"Not...not exactly, but he'll like the idea once he gets used to it."

"Right."

Clay's sardonic tone sparked her defensiveness. "He likes Barry."

"He also likes Rex the Robot on his favorite cartoon show, but he wouldn't want you to marry the guy." Clay jerked his hand through his hair in frustration. "You know, Becca, you're making a big mistake here."

"So you keep telling me."

"You've decided you're going to do this and you're going ahead with it no matter who it hurts."

"That's not true."

"Becca," he said, shaking his head slowly and pinning her with his gaze. "You think I've changed, and maybe I have, but I haven't changed so much that I'll let you do this stupid thing."

"You have no say in it," she flared.

"We'll see."

They stared at each other for a few seconds, his eyes dark green and glittering with determination, hers full of defiance, but she was the one to back down first. With a shake of her head, she turned away, whispering, "Good night, Clay."

She hurried into her room and shut the door, then stood with her fingers pressed to her lips as she waited for the sound of him moving away. It was several minutes before he did, but at last, the house was silent, and Becca relaxed.

Once she was in bed, though, she lay awake for a long time, thinking things over. When she fell asleep, it was to dream troubled dreams.

"Mom. Mom, wake up." A small hand was tapping insistently on her shoulder.

Groggily, Becca opened her eyes and strained to see the small, dark shadow standing beside her bed. "Jimmy?" She pushed herself up on one elbow and shoved her long, loose hair out of her eyes. "What's wrong?"

"I had a bad dream."

She reached out to him. "Oh, I'm so sorry, sweetheart. What was it about?"

As Jimmy climbed into the wide bed beside her, he

told a garbled story about slimy aliens and outer space monsters chasing him. Even in her sleep-fogged state, she knew these characters had come from the forbidden cartoons he and Todd had watched that afternoon.

Becca wrapped her arms around him and hugged him close. "Jimmy, you know those things aren't real."

"I know," he said meekly. "But they still scare me. I need to sleep with you."

Becca blinked and squinted at the clock which said it was three a.m. She started to scoot over to give him a little more room. "Sure, honey," she yawned.

"I need Dad, too."

She froze with one elbow jabbing into the mattress, and her hand grasping the bedcovers. "What?"

"We need to be all three of us," Jimmy said. "I need Dad, too."

"Oh, Jimmy. Dad's sleeping, and...."

"Please, Mom," the little boy insisted, the pitch of his voice raising. "I want Dad, too."

Becca knew there was no reasoning with him when he got that frightened tone. And really, why should she even try? He deserved to have his father there to help him get over a bad dream.

She surrendered without much of a fight. "Okay, honey. I'll go get him." She pulled Jimmy into the center of her bed, tucked him beneath the covers, then tugged on her robe and padded down the hallway. The hardwood floor was cold against her feet, waking her fully.

Quietly, she opened Clay's bedroom door and slipped inside. He lay on his back, the only position in which his cast would allow him to sleep comfortably. His breathing was deep and even.

Becca approached the bed on silent feet and placed her hand on his shoulder. "Clay, wake up."

He didn't stir, so she tried again, shaking him ever so slightly. "Clay," she said softly. She had always hated waking him from a sound sleep. He invariably came awake with a start. For a moment, he would have a wild look in his eyes that would make her wonder what haunted his thoughts in sleep.

Taking a breath, she tried again. "Clay."

"What?" he asked sleepily. His eyes slid open calmly, surprising her, and his hand came up to grasp hers. "What's the matter?"

Becca didn't dwell on this new manifestation of the change in him. Quickly, she explained about Jimmy's nightmare. Clay rose from the bed, fumbled with his crutches and followed her back to her room.

Jimmy was sobbing softly. When his parents came in, he held up his arms. "I thought you weren't coming back."

"We're here now," Clay reassured him.

"Good. Let's all get in together like we used to," the boy demanded, scooting to the exact center of the bed.

Becca's gaze flew to meet Clay's. His face was shadowed in the darkness. He reached down, flipped back the covers, and said, "Whatever you say, son."

She hesitated. "I don't know if that's such a good idea..." she began, but at Jimmy's alarmed cry, she relented. "Okay, okay. Calm down. Let's just see if we can get some sleep."

Her bed was more than large enough for the three of them. Clay lay down on one side of Jimmy, carefully propping his leg on an extra pillow and she lay down on the other. Jimmy snuggled down between them, taking one of their hands in each of his. "Now I can sleep," he said firmly. "With no bad dreams."

He placed their hands on his tummy where they could both feel his breathing and the beat of his heart as he got over his fright and fell quietly back to sleep. Becca tried to move her hand away so she could turn on her side, but he stirred and whimpered so she left it where it was.

Resigned to sleeping in the stiff position, she lay on her back staring at the ceiling.

The three of them had lain like this many times when Jimmy had been sick or frightened. It was rare moments like these that she had always treasured the most, when there was nothing special going on, just the three of them safe and secure together. It seemed that there had been fewer and fewer of those moments in the last months of her marriage to Clay, until they'd stopped altogether.

She listened for Clay's breathing to grow deep and even as Jimmy's had done, but he seemed to be having as much trouble falling back to sleep as she was. She wondered if his leg was hurting, but when he spoke, he didn't seem to be suffering. His voice was low and reflective.

"This is a nice room, Becca."

"Why, thank you," she answered in surprise.

"In fact, the whole house is nice. I guess I never told you, but I appreciated the way you always fixed up the places we lived."

Becca blinked. "No, you never said that before. I didn't think you really noticed."

"I noticed." His voice was deep and firm enough to tell her he was being sincere.

Becca was touched, but she didn't know what to say. She didn't want to tell him that his gratitude and appreciation came too late. That this was what she had needed to hear a few years ago. She didn't need to say anything, though, because after a few minutes he went on.

"No one in my family was the type to fix things up, make a place look like a real home."

Becca breathed slowly, but quietly so she could clearly hear what he was saying. He'd said so little about his family in years past that she didn't want to miss anything he told her now.

"My mother liked to be on the move. It was years before I realized that she was usually one jump ahead of the law."

"Why? What did she do?"

"I don't know. I've never really wanted to know if she was on drugs, or maybe selling them, or, since there were always men around, maybe prostitution...."

"Oh, Clay," Becca said, distressed.

He stopped. Becca wondered if it was because he was afraid Jimmy might wake and hear him.

"Whatever her problems, she was totally self-involved. I don't ever remember being held the way you hold Jimmy."

Tears clogged Becca's throat. "That's horrible, Clay," she choked. "How did you survive until you were taken away and put in a foster home?"

"Kids are resilient. I grew up fast, Becca," he said. "And I suppose I became a cynic at a young age. I knew I couldn't depend on her."

"So you depended solely on yourself," she said quietly.

"Less disappointment that way."

Becca swallowed hard, forcing back the tears. This wasn't the time for them.

She knew now that this was the realization that had

been coming to her for days now, maybe for weeks. Clay kept things to himself because he'd always had to. He'd trusted only himself. Even after their marriage, he'd continued to do that. Becca felt as if she was being stabbed with the twin daggers of disappointment and anger. Why couldn't he have trusted her? If he'd really loved her, wouldn't he have trusted her?

She wanted to ask these questions, but she, too, was aware of Jimmy lying between them. Tomorrow she would ask them. She would get the answers face-to-face because this was one of the reasons their marriage had failed. He hadn't been able to open up to her, and her love for him hadn't been enough of a key to force him to open up to her. Even though he seemed to have changed and she'd certainly learned things about him she hadn't known before, she wasn't sure that made much of a difference.

But for tonight, she needed some moment of closure. She sat up and turned to him. "I wish you'd told me this before," she said, carefully leaning across Jimmy to reach Clay. When he saw what she intended, he reached out to her, placing his hand at the back of her head and drawing her in.

"I couldn't, Becca," he whispered, his breath puffing against her lips. "This kind of thing has always been harder for me than for you."

She answered with a quick nod and let her lips settle onto his. He was warm and vital, and though he'd kissed her twice before in the days since he'd been at her house, he'd been teasing or testing her. Now he was tenderly enjoying her. Becca could feel it in the way he relaxed his jaw, in the pressure of his lips.

Delighted with the pleasure of it, she increased the pressure of her own lips, showing him how much she enjoyed his touch and taste. She refused to allow her mind to make comparisons between Clay and Barry.

Becca allowed all the tenderness she felt to flow out, knowing she was in control of this kiss, that she could relax and let it go only as far as she wanted it to.

At least that's what she thought until Clay put a hand on her shoulder and drew her gently away. "Honey," he said. "Unless you want to move our son to his own bed and let this reach it's natural conclusion, you'd better stop now."

Becca moved away, feeling heat wash up her throat and face, glad the darkness prevented him from seeing her. "Oh, of course." She cleared her throat. "Well, good night, Clay."

"Good night, Becca." His voice was full of humor, but it was laced with tenderness.

Becca lay down, smiling. When Clay reached again for her hand, she didn't hesitate to lace her fingers with his and let them rest on Jimmy's knees. She drifted to sleep with the thought that she felt a closer emotional connection to Clay in this moment than she had at any time during their marriage.

CHAPTER NINE

"WAKE up, Mom."

Becca groaned and hunched her shoulder to ward off the demanding little voice and hands that were shaking her.

"Mom, come on. Open your eyes."

"I can't," she mumbled into her pillow. "Somebody stapled them shut."

He giggled. "Nuh-uh. Wake up."

Eyes still closed, she lifted her head. "Jimmy, this had better be good if you're waking me up twice in one night."

"It's not night anymore, Mom," her son informed her cheerfully. "It's morning. I'm hungry. Can I have some scrambled eggs and some bacon? Maybe some cinnamon toast, too?"

Becca managed to pry one eye open enough to see her son's cheerful face. He always woke ravenous. "Are you sure you want all that to eat?"

He nodded vigorously. "Sure. My bad dreams made me hungry."

"No kidding."

"Will, you, Mom? Will you make me some bacon and eggs? I can make the toast by myself. If you're too sleepy, I could cook the bacon and...."

"Don't you dare touch that stove," Becca warned.

"Oh, okay," he said with a long-suffering sigh.

Becca yawned. The last thing she wanted to do was get up and cook, but she couldn't disappoint him. "I'll

155

fix breakfast for you in a minute.'' She blinked and focused on the clock. "Go get ready for school.''

"Okay." He clambered to the end of the bed and bounced to the floor, then pounded from the room. Becca groaned again.

"Quit sounding like you've got a hangover, Bec.''

"Oh!'' Her eyes popped open and her head tossed on the pillow. "Clay,'' she said. "I'd forgotten about you.''

Moving his casted leg carefully, he turned to face her. He raised himself on one elbow. His dark auburn hair was tousled, his sleepy eyes full of mischief, which seemed to be the usual state with him lately. "Well, it's not the first time, honey.''

"Clay, don't start that.'' She lifted her head and looked toward the lace-curtained window. The sun was just coming up in a cloudless sky. "It's going to be a beautiful day. Don't spoil it.''

His face was full of innocence. "Me? Why, I would never give you a hard time, Becca.''

"Uh-huh,'' she said skeptically. Grasping the covers, she started to toss them back but was hit with a momentary attack of shyness. She knew it was silly. After all, she wasn't a prude and she *had* been married to him. On the other hand, this was hardly the same man she'd known before.

She pondered what he'd told her the night before and knew that she really didn't know him at all. From nowhere came the thought that if she didn't get to know this new Clay better, she would always regret it.

Telling herself not to be foolish, she prepared to swing her legs out of bed. When she tried to stand, though, something held her fast. She bounced onto the mattress and looked back to see that one of Clay's hands was wrapped around the hem of her long, flannel nightgown which had trailed out behind her.

"Clay, let go," she insisted, grasping the thick fabric with both hands and giving it a mighty pull.

His grasp didn't loosen as he shook his head. "As our son would say, Nuh-uh."

She tried to jerk herself free, but he wouldn't release her. "Stop fooling around!"

He grinned. "Now, Becca, fooling around is definitely not what I'm doing here—unless you're issuing an invitation."

She rolled her eyes at him and tried another strategy as she heaved on the nightgown. "Clay, Jimmy's hungry. I've got to fix him some breakfast."

"You can fix me some, too, but not right now."

"You're going to make me late for work."

"Think you might get fired?" he asked in a hopeful tone.

"I *think* you'd better let go of me."

He just grinned, tugged on her nightgown, and brought her, stumbling and struggling down onto the bed beside him.

She bounced against him and cried in alarm, "Clay, your leg."

"Is fine." He held her firmly.

She squeaked in protest, but he cheerfully ignored her demands and said, "It's possible that I had the wrong take on this flannel nightgown thing."

"What do you mean?" She shoved at his hands which he had somehow looped around her waist. "You've always hated them."

He wouldn't let go. How could she have been married to him for five years and not have known he was as tenacious as a pit bull?

He held her with one arm and plucked at the fabric with his other hand. "I always thought they were ugly—big circus tent things, and all that lace they put around the neck and the sleeves looked stupid. I mean, why try to dress up a circus tent?"

"I really wouldn't know," she panted. "Let me go."

He ignored her. "I figured they were okay for a woman who looks like a sumo wrestler, but for a woman built like you, nicely rounded, small waist, nice little bu...." He glanced toward Jimmy's room. "Behind," he amended. "Well, it just seemed like a shame to cover all that up," he concluded in a chatty tone.

Surprise brought Becca's struggles to a stop. She tilted her head back and stared at him. "Clay, what in the world are you talking about?"

"I hated for you to wear them, but now I see that they have a certain mysterious charm all their own." He smoothed the pink-sprigged fabric over her stomach, sending it into an exciting little cha-cha.

"Mysterious charm?" Laughter hitched in her throat.

"Yeah, I think that describes it."

"Crazy describes you."

He smirked. "Oh, please, your compliments will turn my head."

Becca turned her face away to keep from laughing at his coy expression. She wondered again at this stranger. Why couldn't he have been like this when they were married? She had never doubted that he desired her. It had been obvious in the way he had made love to her, but he'd never been playful like this.

As if his teasing wasn't enough to throw her off balance, the feel of his arms around her was doing wild things to her system. Even as she wrestled and fought him, she wanted to lie back and relax, to put her arms around him, hold him close, love him.

But she didn't want this, she thought on a burst of panic. These feelings, this situation weren't at all what she had planned, what she wanted. She quickly returned to the task of trying to pry his hands apart. "That's great, Clay. I'm thrilled you've come to terms with flannel nightgowns. Now let go of me."

"Quit wiggling so I can concentrate."

She managed to pull up two of his fingers and wedge her own in between. Now if she could just break his hold. She panted as she struggled. "You seem to be concentrating just fine."

"Now, where was I?" he asked in a reflective tone.

"You were about to stop this nonsense and let me go fix Jimmy some breakfast."

Clay's eyes narrowed thoughtfully. "No, I don't think that was it. Oh, I remember."

"Goody."

"I was telling you that I've always thought flannel nightgowns are unbecoming."

"They're warm. Something that's very necessary in Colorado in the wintertime. I like to be warm, okay?"

"Fine by me, honey." His hand slid further up her hip and cupped her bottom. "In fact, I think warm is exactly the right word."

In the struggle, Becca's nightgown had slid up above her knees. Clay moved his hand down and reached below the hemline. He touched the skin of her thigh, making Becca jump, then go still once again. Had his touch always been that vital, that compelling?

She lifted her eyes to his. His tone of voice might have been playful, but his eyes were slumberous, his smile sexy.

"Yeah," he said softly. "I think warm is the right word."

Oh, yes. It certainly was. She was pressed up against him, held to his side, pulled halfway over him so that she tingled with his warmth in every place where they touched.

What had they been talking about? It took her a moment to recall. "Warm?" she repeated.

"You just said that," he pointed out. Now his hands were across her back, around her rib cage, drawing her closer. "And you're right. It's very warm. At least as far as I can tell, and I've discovered that they can add a certain intriguing quality to a woman's body."

She blinked at him. "They what?"

He bit his lip. "The flannel nightgowns. They have a certain intriguing quality."

"Along with a mysterious air?"

"Sure. It gives great scope to the imagination to try and picture exactly what a woman looks like underneath. It's actually far more intriguing than a see-through nightie would be."

"You're nuts," Becca said, but she felt a grin twitching at her lips.

"Possibly," he agreed. "After all, I've been sleeping down the hall from you for three weeks and you...." His fingers curled into the soft cotton fabric. "You've been here, wearing this. If only I'd known," he concluded sadly.

"You poor thing," she sympathized.

"On the other hand," he said, cheering up. "I don't have to use my imagination. I only have to tap into my memory." He ran his hand over her back and pulled her close. "Which, by the way, is quite good," he added.

A shiver ran through her and all the fight drained out.

He didn't have to hold her now. She lay along the length of him. His desire for her was obvious, but he wasn't forcing her. His arms eased, the muscles relaxing. She could have scooted away, stood, rushed into the bathroom, cranked up the shower full-blast and as cold as well water in March could be. She didn't move.

Very slowly, his eyes on hers, he lowered his head and lightly brushed her mouth with his. "Imagination's not always a good thing, Becca."

Her lips fell open as his whispered across them again. "It's not?"

"No. In fact, my imagination has been giving me a hell of a time lately."

"That...that's too bad," she said.

"I've been picturing you with Barry."

"You have?"

His jaw rubbed her cheek, making her skin tingle. "Since I'm not into self-torture, it's not something I like to think about."

"I...I can see why not."

"Can you now?" he asked in a voice brimming with approval for her perceptiveness. "Why don't you put an end to my fevered imaginings, Becca?"

Her eyes were trying to drift shut. She wanted to float along in a sweet little cocoon of his voice, his touch, his kisses. "How can I do that, Clay?"

"You can tell me you've never slept with Barry."

A chill swept through her. Her eyes opened. "What?"

"I don't think you have, but I'd like to know for sure." The teasing was gone from his eyes. His expression was serious and intense as if he was willing her to give him the answer he wanted. "I know you're engaged to him, but I also know you. I think you'd probably wait until you married him."

His practical words went a long way toward snagging her out of the languorous haze in which she'd been drifting. "Clay, that's none of your business."

"And if I had a nickel for every time you've said that in the past few weeks, I'd be a very rich man," he answered sardonically. "Can't you just tell me?"

Oh, why was she fighting it? He wouldn't stop until he heard the answer he wanted. She sighed. "No. No, I haven't slept with him." She'd been uncomfortable with the thought of being intimate with Barry in her house where Jimmy would have been just down the hall. She hadn't felt much better about the idea of leaving her son overnight with a member of her family while she'd been at Barry's apartment. Barry hadn't pushed the issue and she'd been touched by his gentlemanliness.

Clay smiled then and it held a mixture of triumph and tenderness. His head dipped once again. "Good girl," he said just before his lips took hers. Somehow, she tasted that same triumph, that same tenderness in his kiss. She didn't respond, but he didn't seem to mind. After a moment, he drew back and looked at her as if he knew what she would say next, that she wouldn't marry Barry because she was still in love with Clay.

When she said nothing, he seemed to take it philosophically. "You know, Becca, for the past three weeks we've been talking about things we should have talked about a long time ago, but only in bits and pieces."

"What do you mean?"

"We never really talked about the miscarriages or about your father's death. I was waiting for you to heal enough to talk about them, but you never did. Instead, you started changing, toward me, toward our marriage."

"So you said," she answered dryly. Her tone was sardonic to hide the distress she felt. She wasn't sure she was ready to talk about this even now. If they never brought it out into the open, it would be possible for her to continue thinking that the majority of their problems had been Clay's fault. Immediately on the heels of that thought came a wash of shame. He was absolutely right. She had been running, ducking, and hiding for ages now and she was so tired of it.

"Becca, I grieved for your father, too. He was a great guy. Watching him showed me what kind of father I wanted to be."

Tears flooded into Becca's eyes. "Oh, Clay. I didn't know. You never said."

"No, I didn't, and I'm sorry I didn't tell him." Clay paused, his dark green eyes swirling with regret and sorrow. "I grieved for the daughters we lost, too, but I felt worse for you because you'd never had such a loss before."

"Clay, I lost my mother when I was two."

"But you don't remember her, do you? And you had Mary Jane as your mother from the time you were six. No, because you're from such a strong family, lots of people around to help you through a crisis, you never had to depend only on yourself, find strength inside to deal with the losses you suffered."

"And you did. You had to." Recalling what she'd learned about him in the past few weeks, things she'd never known before, Becca felt sick at the way she had misjudged him. He had cared about the losses they had suffered, but because he didn't show it the way she thought he should, she had thought he didn't care.

"Yes, Becca, I had to, and now it's time for you to find that strength to do what's right."

In spite of the deep shame she was feeling, Becca

wasn't sure she could face up to what he was expecting of her. "I don't know, Clay...."

"You've let this situation go on long enough," he said. "Hell, *I've* let it go on long enough."

She knew exactly what he meant. Barry, and her engagement to him. She needed to face it, to deal with it, but she was so overwhelmed by everything that had happened to her in the past twelve hours, she also needed time to handle things in her own way.

He was watching her expectantly, but all she could do was plead softly, "Oh, Clay, please don't do this. Don't push me like this."

He didn't have to ask what she meant. He put his hand under her jaw and tilted her head up. "I have to, Becca. I have to take whatever opportunities I can."

"No."

"Yes." His voice was firm, unflinching. "I went along with the divorce because I thought it was what you wanted, maybe even what would be best for Jimmy, but I was wrong. I should have fought it."

"You *did* fight it."

"Not hard enough. I still want you. That will never change. You can make all the plans you want to marry another man, but you're my wife. That's not going to change."

Alarm shot through her. "It *has* changed," she said fiercely. "Everything's changed. It's too late to go back—not that I would want to."

"Sounds like you're trying to convince yourself, not me."

"Clay," she said, shaking her head frantically. "You're impossibly stubborn."

He snorted derisively. "*I'm* not the one who's being

stubborn. You're refusing to see a truth that's staring you right in the face."

She started to answer, but Jimmy called out from the doorway. "Hey, are you two wrestling? Can I play?" He dashed to the bed and started to climb up, but Becca moved away from Clay, tugging fiercely on her nightgown until he let go.

"No," Clay said, looking at Jimmy. "We were just talking."

Jimmy's face crumpled in disappointment. He'd made a slapdash effort at washing his face. Water still dripped down his cheek and onto the shoulder of his T-shirt. He gave his parents a suspicious frown. "Looked like wrestling to me."

"We'll wrestle another time, son," Clay answered. "Right now, your mom's going to fix some breakfast. Why don't you get your comb and let me see if I can straighten out your part?" He wiped the water from Jimmy's cheek, then touched his hair where the part zigzagged like a mountain railroad track. Over the boy's head, he gave Becca a long, serious look.

She answered with a distressed shake of her head, whirled away and hurried for the bathroom. Everything seemed to be rushing in on her. To her shame, she acknowledged that she was letting things happen. She wasn't creating her own future, or even planning it. She was only standing by and watching her life take place. The one thing in the past year or so that she had planned and created was the divorce and she now knew that had been the wrong thing to do, because no matter what she told herself, she was still in love with Clay Saunders.

"Well, how do you think it's going, Becca?"

Becca started when Barry touched her arm and whispered in her ear. It took her a moment to focus on his question. His parents had met them at the restaurant in Durango for lunch. After they had eaten, they returned to Barry's apartment in Tarrant for coffee. Now they were discussing the places they would like to visit that afternoon. The Whelkers appeared to be avid sight-seers. This was only their second trip to southern Colorado and they were anxious to view as many points of interest as possible.

"I think it's going fine, Barry," Becca answered. The two of them were in his tiny kitchen, trying to maneuver around each other as they prepared the coffee tray. "Your parents are very nice."

She winced inwardly at that bland statement. The truth was, they *were* nice—to Jimmy, but they viewed her with reservations or suspicion. Becca hadn't quite decided which it was.

"I think they like you."

Becca wanted to ask how he could tell since they'd hardly spoken to her all through lunch, though they listened to everything she said as if she was a spy telling state secrets. Or perhaps they knew at first glance that she was a weak and vacillating woman who didn't know her own mind and they were trying to think of a way to warn their son away from her, she thought guiltily.

"Becca," Barry prompted. "I think they like you."

She couldn't imagine why. Right now, she didn't even like herself very much.

Her smile was wooden as she said, "That's good."

Of course it was possible that she was reading too much into their attitude. After all, she was sure she and Clay would react the same way when their son invited them to meet the girl he planned to marry.

She and Clay. She thought of herself with him as if

the two of them were still a couple, were still married. What he had said that morning was true. She was still his wife. No matter what she had told herself in the past year, it was true.

With nervous little gestures, she arranged and rearranged cups, saucers, sugar bowl and creamer on the tray. She added a glass of cold orange soda pop for Jimmy. Her hand fell to rest on the counter. It was a measure of Barry's thoughtfulness that he even had orange soda on hand. He didn't care for it, but he knew Jimmy did.

Slowly, over the past couple of days, she had begun to acknowledge something she hadn't been willing to admit before. Barry was a good friend, certainly the best male friend she'd ever had, and that was exactly the way she loved him. His thoughtfulness and consideration had been things she'd desperately needed after she had left Clay. He had helped restore her faith in herself and she would always be grateful to him for that, but friendship and gratitude weren't a basis for a marriage.

It made her physically ill to do so, but she had to admit she had been doggedly pursuing her plans to marry Barry because it was easier than dealing with her feelings for Clay.

How had she gotten herself into this mess? she wondered, but she already knew the answer. She'd gotten herself into this mess because she had drifted into it. Instead of dealing with things head-on, she had thought things would resolve themselves, freeing her from taking the responsibility of making the decision herself.

Even after she had realized early yesterday morning that she was still in love with Clay, she had let things drift. Amazingly, he hadn't pushed her even though he must have known the quandary she was in. He watched her as if he was waiting for her to do something. No doubt, he was giving her enough rope to hang herself, she thought morosely. He hadn't even objected when Barry had picked up her and Jimmy late that morning to meet Barry's parents.

To her shame, she didn't know what to do. Yes, she was still in love with Clay, but that didn't mean they could work things out and make a life together, even if they both wanted to. After all, they'd tried it before.

But she hadn't known things about him then that she knew now, her conscience prompted.

And, there was the question of Barry. He had been so good to her, so patient and understanding, especially over the matter of Clay living with her while he recovered from his injuries. She couldn't bear to hurt his feelings by breaking her engagement, but she also couldn't marry him. It wouldn't be fair to either of them.

She had planned to tell him so yesterday at work, but it had been one of those days in which nothing seemed to work the way she wanted. He'd been busy all day, they couldn't seem to get out of the office together for lunch, and Hope Bishop had been ever-present. Today, they hadn't been alone for a moment and it wasn't news she could deliver in front of her son or his parents.

"Are you coming?"

She started again and looked up. Barry stood in the doorway with the coffee carafe in his hands. He frowned at her. "Are you okay, Rebecca?"

"Yes," she said hastily. "I'm just...." She couldn't even think of a word to describe the state she was in.

"Nervous?" He smiled with understanding. "It's okay. They don't bite."

She answered with a sickly smile of her own and followed him into the living area. They had their coffee and Jimmy drank a little of his orange soda before he set his cup down and began to wander through Barry's apartment. He had many books and a new computer that she knew Jimmy was dying to touch. Barry wasn't obsessive about his things, but he was neat and she wasn't sure he would appreciate her son's meddling.

The stilted conversation continued among the adults while Becca kept one eye on her son's activities. He was standing in front of Barry's desk, with his arms resting on the back of the chair and his eyes gazing longingly at the screen. She hoped he wouldn't ask to play games on it. She doubted that Barry had any and certainly not ones a six-year-old could play. Besides, she doubted that he'd want Jimmy playing computer games when there were guests sitting only a few feet away.

"....your collection of glassware, Becca."

Hearing her name, she glanced up. "Excuse me?"

"Mother collects glassware, too," Barry said.

Becca smiled as her gaze slid sideways to her son. "How nice."

"I'm sure I've mentioned that," Barry went on, looking as if he wondered why she wasn't paying closer attention. He stood to begin gathering the coffee things.

Reacting automatically to the disappointment in his tone, Becca said, "Oh, oh, yes. Of course." She tried frantically to recall what he'd told her. She'd been so distracted over the situation with Clay for the past few weeks, she was doing well to remember her own name. "Rose-patterned plates, isn't it? And pink Depression glass? My glassware is mostly from the twenties. Some of it belonged to my great-grandmother." She glanced over and saw Jimmy reaching for the switch on the computer. Rising immediately, she went to him. Bending close, she whispered, "Jimmy, honey, please don't touch that."

He started and gave her a guilty look. His bottom lip stuck out. "There's nothing to do here. I wanna go home."

"We'll go pretty soon."

"I would love to see it," Mrs. Whelker said.

There was a moment of silence before Becca realized the other woman was speaking to her. She glanced around. "See what?"

"Your pre-Depression glassware. I'd love to see it."

"Mom, I wanna go home," Jimmy whined.

"Hey, we could do both," Mr. Whelker broke in. "Take the little guy home and see this glass you girls are so crazy about, then head back to our hotel."

Becca sent Barry a pleading look, but his back was turned as he walked into the kitchen area.

She glanced around, feeling trapped, and met the Whelkers' puzzled expressions. Here she was, once again, drifting into a situation. She couldn't think of any way to politely refuse. It would hurt Barry, and she was going to hurt him enough when she broke their engagement.

She cleared her throat. "Oh, well, I suppose that would be fine." She knew she sounded far less than enthusiastic, but she really didn't want them to meet Clay and wonder what kind of woman she was, but she also didn't want to be rude. Her smile was thin when she said, "Why don't we do that?"

When Barry returned from the kitchen, she told him the plan, her eyes pleading with him to understand. He gave her a long, hard look before he turned to go into his bedroom to retrieve their coats.

When they were on their way with his parents following in their own car, Barry took his eyes off the road for a moment. He gave her another searching look before turning his attention back to his driving. "What's going on, Becca?"

She glanced over her shoulder at Jimmy, who was playing with a small toy he'd found in his pocket. "Barry, we need to talk."

"We're on our way to your house where my parents are going to meet your ex-husband who's in residence, has been in residence for weeks, and who doesn't show any signs of vacating the place. I think we should have talked before we got to this point," he said, with heat in his voice.

Shocked by his vehemence, Becca shot back, "You thought it was a good idea for me to care for him."

"Yes, but I didn't think you were going to *care* for him, if you know what I mean. The idea was for you to get over him, not pick up where you left off." He glanced in the rearview mirror at Jimmy, who had stopped playing and was watching them from the back seat.

"Barry, I...I haven't," she stammered.

Barry started to answer, but when Jimmy shifted in his seat and leaned forward, he only muttered, "We'll have to talk about this later."

By the time they pulled into her driveway and parked behind Clay's Explorer, Becca felt as if she was heading for an inevitable confrontation. Her only prayer was to get through this as gracefully as possible and talk to Barry in private as soon as she could.

To her relief, Clay wasn't in evidence when they entered the house. Becca hoped he was in his room and would stay there until her guests left.

She had expected Jimmy to head straight for his room,

or to go to Todd's house, but he seemed curiously reluctant to leave her. He tagged along behind her when she led Mrs. Whelker into the dining room and then into the kitchen where they shared what they found appealing about antique glass. Though the men didn't have much interest in it, they tagged along to the kitchen. Jimmy wrapped himself around her waist, throwing her off balance, and wouldn't let go.

Mrs. Whelker began to warm to her at that point. "I'm so glad you have a real interest in domestic things," she said. "Susan certainly didn't."

Over his mother's shoulder, Becca caught an alarmed look on Barry's face and wondered what had caused it. "Susan?" she asked.

"Barry's former fiancée." The lady gave her son a sympathetic look. "She certainly broke their engagement just before he moved here. She also broke his heart. I'm sure he told you about her."

Becca blinked. This was the first she'd heard of a fiancée. "Uh, well, no. We've never actually discussed her."

"That's in the past, Mother," Barry put in.

"Oh, I know. I just want you to find happiness, and I didn't think you would with her. She wasn't ready to settle down, but Rebecca here, has already established a home of her own. That's very encouraging."

Before anyone could respond to this ringing endorsement, Becca heard a familiar thumping noise cross the living room and come toward the kitchen. With a sinking dread and the instinct of a hunted animal sensing danger, she turned to see Clay approaching the doorway.

When he reached it, he stood, leaning on his crutches and surveying the group in the kitchen. He examined each person and smiled briefly at his son who still clung to Becca's waist, before bringing his attention back to fix steadily on Becca.

"You didn't tell me we were going to have company, Becca," he said in a mild tone. She would have thought his words were mocking if she hadn't seen the sympathy on his face. He knew what she had done, that she had allowed this situation to develop. He felt sorry for her, but he wasn't going to save her from it.

"Oh, Clay," she said in a strangled voice. "Hello." She lifted her hands in a helpless gesture. "These are Barry's parents." She took a breath that felt as if it was loaded with dull saw blades. "Mr. and Mrs. Whelker, this is my husband, Clay."

In unison, they turned stunned faces to her and she rushed to correct her gaffe. "Sex-husband," she blurted. "I mean, *ex-husband*."

A long, painfully embarrassed silence followed. Clay finally broke it by murmuring, "How do you do?"

"He lives with you here?" Mr. Whelker boomed. "I sure hope you don't plan to have him with you after you and Barry are married."

"No, I...not... He's recovering from a broken leg," she said weakly, indicating his cast. Suddenly tired of being cast as the villain here, even though she knew she was wrong, Becca gave Barry an irritated glance. He could have helped out by telling her parents about Clay. He could help out now, but he just stood there looking uncomfortable.

"My mom's not going to marry him," Jimmy suddenly shouted, making them all jump. Becca whipped around to see his stricken face. He pointed his finger at her. "You better marry my dad." He spun around to face Clay. "You're not going to let her marry him, are you, Dad?"

Clay's eyes swept the room, landing on Becca. "No, son. I'm not."

CHAPTER TEN

CLAY'S quiet statement was followed by a long, awkward silence. Jimmy finally broke it by turning to Barry and his parents.

"You go away now," he said in the high-pitched voice he used when he was excited or upset. "We don't want you here."

Appalled, Becca overreacted. Pulling him away from her, she held him by the shoulders, looked into his face and said, "Jimmy, that was rude! You apologize to our guests."

He stuck his bottom lip out defiantly. "No! They shouldn't be here. It should just be you and me and Dad. I don't like old Barry and you better not marry him. My dad won't like it and he won't let you do it." He broke away from her and ran toward Clay, who reached out for him, but in his distress, Jimmy didn't stop. He barreled past his father, and ran toward his room. The slam of his door echoed through the house.

Shakily, Becca turned to the Whelkers who looked as if they'd rather be anywhere than in her kitchen at that moment. She couldn't blame them. She felt the same way.

"I'm so sorry," she stammered. "My son...."

"I think we'd better go," Barry's mother broke in hastily. "Come along, Fred. Let's be on our way. Barry, are you coming?"

"In a minute, Mother," Barry said. His irritated look told Becca that he wanted to talk to her. Her heart sank because she knew she would deserve whatever he said to her now.

"Suit yourself." Mrs. Whelker headed rapidly for the door, followed by her husband, and Clay swung out of the way to let them pass.

When the front door had snapped shut behind them, he gazed at Becca's stricken face, then at Barry's angry one and said, "Looks like you two need to talk." He turned and left the two of them alone.

"I'm so sorry," Becca said immediately as she turned to face Barry. "I don't know what came over Jimmy...."

"This isn't Jimmy's fault," Barry interrupted angrily. "This is yours. How long have you known you weren't going to marry me? That this whole thing was a farce?"

Shame washed over her. "A couple of days," she answered, unable to meet his eyes.

"Longer than that, I think, but you wouldn't admit it. Here I was going along in a fool's paradise, making plans, and you never intended to go through with marrying me. I was honest with you from the very beginning, but you weren't with me."

Becca held up her hands. "Wait a minute. What about this person named Susan? You never told me about her."

He had the grace to look embarrassed. "All right, I admit maybe I started dating you on the rebound...."

"And maybe proposed to me for the same reason."

"Whatever," he said, throwing his hands out. "Your son's right. Your ex-husband will never let you marry me. And you wouldn't want to anyway, because you're still in love with him." Barry headed for the door. "Well, excuse me, but I'm not interested in being part of a triangle."

Becca winced at his tone. He didn't spare her another

glance, or speak to Clay as he stalked through the living room and out the door, closing it firmly behind him. When the house was quiet, Becca crumpled. Her shoulders sagged and her arms hung limply at her sides. She wanted to go into her room, fall across her bed and give way to tears of frustration and anger, but she needed to talk to Jimmy first, though she didn't know what she was going to say beyond apologizing for being a fool.

Squaring her shoulders, she left the kitchen and started across the living room only to be brought up short by Clay who stood squarely in the middle of the room regarding her with a sardonic expression.

"Can we assume the engagement is off, Becca?"

She lifted a trembling hand. "Why don't you just leave it, Clay? Hasn't enough happened here today?" Her voice broke on the last word and she cursed herself for being a coward. Giving him one desperate look, she abandoned all dignity and ran for the hall.

The tears broke in less than an instant. She veered from Jimmy's closed door to her own room which offered a haven. Dashing inside, she gave the door a haphazard push and threw herself across her bed. She had enough presence of mind to grab a pillow and hold it against her mouth so Jimmy wouldn't hear the great, racking sobs that came from her throat.

She hated what she'd done, for arrogantly thinking she was making all the right decisions when she'd really been making one disastrous mistake after another and Jimmy was the one who was suffering for it. She cried until her eyes were dry, until she was rid of her self-pity.

Finally, she went into the bathroom, washed her face, and repaired her makeup, preparing herself to face Clay and Jimmy. When she came out of her room, she saw that Clay was where she'd left him half an hour before, sitting in the living room, his leg propped on the hassock, his chin in his hand.

When he heard her, he looked up. His green eyes were dark with censure. "If you're finished crying over your fiancé, it's time for us to talk about our son, and to talk to our son. I tried already, but he said he wanted us to leave him alone."

Becca had a great many things she wanted to say to Clay, but she knew they would have to wait until Jimmy was reassured. Without a word to Clay, she turned and knocked on Jimmy's door.

"Jimmy," she called softly. "It's Mom. Can I come in?"

When there was no answer, she opened the door and peeked inside. He wasn't lying on his bed or sitting on the floor surrounded by his military figures. Her gaze swept the room, then she gasped when she spotted the window. It was open in spite of the cool temperature outside and the screen had been removed.

Her heart pounding, she rushed across the room and looked outside. There was no sign of him. A cold shudder ran through her. She was sure he had run away. She dashed to the bathroom, which was also empty.

"Clay!" Whirling around, she rushed back to the living room where her panicked tone had urged Clay to his feet.

"What is it?" he asked, scanning her frantic expression.

"Jimmy. He's gone." Quickly, she told him about the open window and missing screen.

"What else is missing?"

"I...I don't know. I didn't notice."

They hurried back to the bedroom where a quick

check told them their son had taken the old backpack Clay had given him, along with his "mining gear."

Becca stared at Clay, her eyes full of panic. "Where could he have gone?"

"Becca, calm down. Call his friends. See if he's with one of them."

"Oh, of course." Becca rushed to the phone in her bedroom and quickly called her son's friends, but no one had seen him.

Shakily, she hung up the phone and gave Clay a distressed shake of her head.

Supporting himself on one crutch, Clay put his arm around her and drew her close.

She let herself relax against him for a moment as he said, "He's only a small boy. He can't have gotten very far."

"Far or not doesn't matter," she answered, anguished. "He could get hurt a few feet from the house."

"Don't think in terms of him getting hurt," Clay commanded sharply. "Or you really will panic."

With a nod, Becca swallowed the hysteria that was threatening to engulf her. She was grateful for Clay's steadiness and strength. Moving away from him, she pushed her hands through her hair and pressed her palms against her temples. "We've got to think like he would."

"He was pretty upset," Clay pointed out.

Miserably, Becca nodded. She knew that, and she also knew she was responsible for it.

"Why would he have taken his backpack?" Clay asked, half to himself.

"He takes it with him everywhere," she pointed out. "You know that."

"Yes, but he doesn't always take all that stuff he calls his 'mining gear,' does he?"

She straightened. "No. No, he doesn't." The color drained from her face. "Clay, you don't think he...?"

"The Lucy Belle," he concluded grimly.

"Oh, no."

"Remember when we were up there a couple of weeks ago, how he wanted to go inside? He said people could live in there if they didn't have a house."

"But it's two miles from here. He couldn't walk that far."

"Sure he could, if he was mad enough, and in record time, too."

"I guess so." She nodded slowly, her mind forming the image of the yawning dark mouth of the mine opening. "We've got to go look for him," she said. "Maybe if he's headed in that direction, we can still catch up with him. Do you think we should call the search and rescue squad?"

"Let's try on our own first. Too much activity might panic him. If we don't locate him in half an hour, we'll call them."

"Okay. Let's go."

As fast as they could, they climbed into Clay's Explorer and started off. As she drove slowly along the road, they scanned the bar ditches and fields, but saw no sign of him. When they turned up the old road to the mine, Clay shouted, "There!"

Becca stood on the brakes and whipped her head around, searching frantically. She saw only a flash of red. Leaping from the car, she ran to it, snatched it up and cried out. "It's Jimmy's red jacket. He's been this way."

As she threw it into the car and jumped in, Clay said,

"He must have gotten hot while he was walking, taken it off, and dropped it."

Her heart in her throat, she nodded, put the vehicle in low gear, and started up the steep track. She made the climb in record time and screeched to a halt before the mine's entrance.

Piling from the car, she and Clay began shouting for their son. She dashed to the opening while Clay maneuvered laboriously around the strewn boulders. He scrutinized the rough ground for footprints, but shook his head when Becca gave him a questioning look.

"No tracks," he said. "But that doesn't necessarily mean he isn't in there."

"Oh, dear God," she breathed.

"We're going to have to go in after him," Clay said grimly. "Get the flashlight from the car."

Becca did as he said and the two of them started inside, calling softly so that Jimmy wouldn't be frightened by the booming echo of their voices. Hampered by his cast and the crutches, Clay's progress was slow, but neither of them considered quitting.

They were one hundred yards inside the mine, at the place where the ground began to slope downward, when they heard the sound of sobbing.

"Jimmy! Jimmy, answer us. Are you all right?"

"Ye...hes," a quavering voice returned. "Mom? Dad? Is that you?"

"Yes. We're coming, son," Clay called reassuringly. They rounded a small bend. The beam of their flashlight caught their son sitting huddled on the floor, hugging his backpack to him.

When he saw their light, he stood and stumbled toward them. Becca scooped him up and he clutched her neck. Clay dropped one of his crutches and wrapped his arm around them, hugging them close. Becca leaned into him, savoring the moment of relief that their son was safe.

After they had all calmed down a bit, she pulled away, Clay picked up his crutch, and they started slowly from the mine.

Once they were out in the daylight, she unwrapped Jimmy's arms from her neck, held him away, and said, "Jimmy, why did you come up here? What were you thinking?"

He shrugged. "I...I don't know. I was mad at you and I didn't want to live with you anymore, so I came up here to live."

"Oh, Jimmy," she said, shaking her head.

"I was gonna bring food," he said defensively. "But I didn't want you to see me go in the kitchen, so I just left. When I got in the mine, I fell and my flashlight wouldn't work anymore." His lips started to tremble. "I got scared. I wanna go home."

"We're going right now, Jimmy," Clay said. "All three of us."

Becca drove home while Clay held Jimmy who clutched his father tightly. Clay rubbed his back and spoke soothingly to him while Jimmy sobbed out his fright. By the time they reached home, he was exhausted. Becca carried him into the house and laid him on his bed, then they both sat with him until he fell asleep.

When he seemed to be napping soundly, Becca got wearily to her feet. She had been so battered by emotions that she could hardly think. She gave Clay a despairing look and stumbled across the hall to her own room. She fell on her bed once again and for the second time that day, let the tears flow, though these were tears of relief.

Becca knew when Clay came into the room. Even

though she was sure he could hear her crying, he didn't hesitate to nudge the door open with his crutch, then close it behind him.

"Tears won't help now, Becca," he said softly. "He's safe. You don't need to cry."

"Maybe I do," she answered in a muffled voice. "It was my fault he ran off like that." Guilt swamped her. "If something had happened to him...."

Clay approached the bed where she lay huddled. "Don't borrow trouble, Becca. Nothing bad happened except that he got a good fright, which might mean he'll think twice before he does something like that again." He chuckled, but it sounded rusty in his throat. "At least we can hope he'll think twice."

She nodded, then lifted her face to him. Trying for dignity, she said, "I'd like to be left alone for a while, Clay."

His lips tilted in a sympathetic smile, but he shook his head. "Sorry, Becca, I'm afraid I can't do that."

"Go away, Clay. Would you, for once, leave me alone?"

He shook his head, his eyes steady and determined. "No, as a matter of fact, I won't. You've been through a bad time today, and like it or not, you need me."

"I *need* to be left alone," she said stubbornly.

"I left you alone when you were suffering after your father died. I left you alone each time when you miscarried. I thought you needed that. I thought you needed that time to heal. I was wrong. I should have forced you to talk to me, made you face it and get over it."

"I don't need you to psychoanalyze me," she said frostily.

"I'm not. I'm analyzing myself." He came and sat beside her on the bed, then easing his casted leg up, he settled against the headboard. "I didn't push myself into your grief and make you come to terms with it because I didn't know I was supposed to."

"What do you mean?"

"Think about it, Becca. I spent my life running away from emotions—ducking my mother's drunken rages, trying not to care when I was jerked from one foster home to another." He looked down, spread his hands, then closed them into fists. "I didn't know how to deal with grief as deep as yours when Hal died, when you miscarried. I'd never had to face anything as hard as watching you suffer."

Her eyes on his, Becca sat up. Her absolute surprise at his words made her face go blank as she said, "You seemed so...cold. I didn't know what you were thinking."

He winced. "I know. It was a shell I built around myself to keep from feeling too deeply. I figured out when I was about Jimmy's age that letting people see inside you only invited pain." His lips tightened and he drew in a breath. "But I didn't know what true pain was until you took him and left."

"But you only seemed angry."

"I was furious and I stayed that way for months." He gave her a self-mocking look. "I'm a slow learner. It took me that long to decide that it was my own fault you'd left, but it didn't help that you *had* left. You weren't there to fight out the problems with me, find a solution."

"I was as much at fault as you were, Clay," she admitted.

"Maybe so. We're both pretty hardheaded. When I found out you intended to marry Barry, I saw red. I couldn't believe I was really going to lose you. Then the accident happened. When I woke up in the hospital and saw you, the worry on your face, I felt hopeful for the first time in more than a year. I knew I had to lose the anger and win you back. The broken leg gave me the opportunity to do that. For the first time in my life I could relax and let things develop. I didn't have to push or worry, or plan.''

"You charmed me," she said, smiling. "I couldn't resist your humor and teasing and warmth.''

"Yeah, warm and charming." He wiggled his eyebrows at her. "It was a tactic I hadn't tried.''

"It worked.''

She lifted her hands helplessly. "I didn't think you were interested in finding one.''

"I was interested," he said gruffly, reaching for her. "I'm still interested. If you are.''

A sob caught in her throat. "Yes. Yes, of course I am.''

He pulled her to him then and his mouth covered hers, telling her of the tortures he'd been through, wanting her as badly as she wanted him. He pulled away to say in a raw voice, "I never stopped loving you, Becca, even when I didn't show you how much I loved you.''

"Oh, Clay," she answered in a shaking voice. "I never stopped loving you, either. I was so selfish, concentrating only on myself. I thought I was doing what was best for myself and for Jimmy, but I was running away. I used the excuse that I wanted to stay in one place, to have a real home, but that was only a small part of it. Things weren't as perfect between us as I thought they should be, so I ran. Even after five years, I had an unrealistic idea of what marriage should be. When it didn't turn out like I thought it should, I ran. I was so wrong. I should have stayed to work things out.''

Clay kissed her again. "Yeah, I never figured you for a quitter."

"I never figured me for one, either," she admitted.

They talked for an hour, sorting through the false expectations they'd had of each other. All the time, Clay held her and she clung to him. This, at last, was what she'd wanted from him; this openness and understanding. Now that she was experiencing it, she felt a deepening of her love for him.

At last, Clay placed his fist under her chin and turned her face up to him. He smiled at her, and in his eyes, she saw everything she'd hoped for. He lowered his mouth to hers, kissing her long and deep. She felt once again the surge of excitement she had always known with him. She put her arms around him and kissed him back, showing all the love and fervor she felt.

At last, he said, "You know what this means, don't you?"

"No, what?"

"You're going to have to marry me again. I think it's just possible that we might get everything right this time."

"Oh?" she asked on a shaky laugh. "What makes you think so?"

"Our son will force us to, for one thing."

"That's true."

Becca leaned against his shoulder, feeling the warmth and comfort she'd always longed for coupled with his fervent desire for her.

"Lucky you. You'll be Jimmy's hero for not letting me marry Barry."

Clay sat back and gave her a self-satisfied grin. "I thought I was his hero already."

They laughed together, then Clay grew thoughtful. "I can't give up the way I make a living, Becca."

She swallowed hard. More moves, she thought, but this time she didn't feel the dread she'd always known before. He was a different man now, and she was a different woman. "I know," she answered. "And I don't expect you to."

"But I could change it."

"How?"

"These old mines," he said thoughtfully. "The west is riddled with them. There's got to be a better way of closing them off, of protecting the public than just posting No Trespassing signs."

She sat up and looked at him. There was a deep interest and excitement in his eyes.

"What have you got in mind?"

"I could start my own company," he said. "We could contract out to the mine owners, local governments, and develop ways of closing them off. The owners would want to save money on the safeguards, but I think I could do it. I'd like to try. My base of operations could be right here in Tarrant. I'd be home most nights, and every weekend."

Becca put her arms around his neck. "Mister, that's an offer I can't refuse."

Laughing, he kissed her again. "Thank God. I was hoping you'd let me stick around. I'm glad I won't have to put Plan B into operation."

She drew back and looked at the sparkle in his eyes; the sparkle she'd come to love. "Oh, what was Plan B?"

He put his lips close to her ear and whispered, "Breaking my other leg."

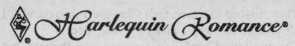

Invites You to A Wedding!

Whirlwind Weddings
Combines the heady
romance of a whirlwind
courtship with the
excitement of a wedding—
strong heroes, feisty
heroines and marriages
made not so much in
heaven as in a hurry!

What's the catch? All our heroes and heroines meet
and marry within a week! Mission impossible?
Well, a lot can happen in seven days....

January 1998—#3487 MARRY IN HASTE
by Heather Allison

February 1998—#3491 DASH TO THE ALTAR
by Ruth Jean Dale

March 1998—#3495 THE TWENTY-FOUR-HOUR BRIDE
by Day Leclaire

April 1998—#3499 MARRIED IN A MOMENT
by Jessica Steele

Who says you can't hurry love?

Available wherever Harlequin books are sold.

This April
DEBBIE MACOMBER

takes readers to the Big Sky and beyond...

MONTANA

At her grandfather's request, Molly packs up her kids and returns to his ranch in Sweetgrass, Montana.

But when she arrives, she finds a stranger, Sam Dakota, working there. Molly has questions: What exactly is he doing there? Why doesn't the sheriff trust him? Just *who* is Sam Dakota? These questions become all the more critical when her grandfather tries to push them into marriage....

Moving to the state of Montana is one thing; entering the state of matrimony is quite another!

Available in April 1998 wherever books are sold.

MIRA

MDM434

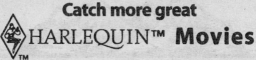

HARLEQUIN ULTIMATE GUIDES™

A series of how-to books for today's woman.

Act now to order some of these extremely
helpful guides just for you!

*Whatever the situation, Harlequin Ultimate Guides™
has all the answers!*

Welcome to *Love Inspired*™

A brand-new series of contemporary inspirational love stories.

Join men and women as they learn valuable lessons about facing the challenges of today's world and about life, love and faith.

**Look for the following April 1998
Love Inspired™ titles:**

DECIDEDLY MARRIED
by Carole Gift Page

A HOPEFUL HEART
by Lois Richer

HOMECOMING
by Carolyne Aarsen

Available in retail outlets in March 1998.

LIFT YOUR SPIRITS AND GLADDEN YOUR HEART
with *Love Inspired!*™

Steeple
Hill™

LI498